"The pity routine got you, didn't it?"

"Not a chance." Teddi smiled up at him. "I love your body," she said softly. She loved the long, graceful lines, the sharp definition of muscle and sinew and his craggy face.

Rising on an elbow, she offered her mouth for a lingering kiss, feeling at ease for the first time since she'd set foot in Colorado. She decided she could fall asleep in about two blissful minutes. "Teddi?"

"Hmm?" The blizzard howled around the corners of the house, but it didn't frighten her. Not now. She felt safe and warm and protected. Nothing could hurt her here.

"Isn't it time we talked about it?"

Her eyes flew open. She sat bolt upright and stared at him. "No! I'm—" She bit off the words and examined his calm, expectant expression. He was watching her. And waiting.

Suddenly she felt trapped.

ABOUT THE AUTHOR

Early in life, Margaret St. George set two goals: to publish a book and to be ravished by Burt Reynolds. Obviously she has achieved her first goal; she has not given up hope on the second. This is Margaret's seventh novel, though most of her books have been historical romances. She lives with her husband and family in Colorado.

Winter Magic

MARGARET ST. GEORGE

Harlequin Books

TORONTO • NEW YORK • LONDON
AMSTERDAM • PARIS • SYDNEY • HAMBURG
STOCKHOLM • ATHENS • TOKYO • MILAN

Published March 1986

First printing January 1986

ISBN 0-373-16142-5

Chapter One

Fat puffs of snow tumbled out of the night sky and floated past the lodge window. Teddi Ansel stared at the flakes melting against the panes, and her throat dried.

Returning to Vail had been a mistake.

Leaning forward, she steadied herself against the windowsill and battled the unwanted images storming through her memory: rumbling snow... cold... icy white... and deadly.

So deadly.

Closing her eyes, Teddi turned away from the drifting snow, momentarily surrendering to an onslaught of dizziness. It would have been wiser to remain in safe, warm Lahaina, on the island of Maui, where June lasted all year and residents joked about blizzards on the mainland.

Shivering against the cold leaking from the window, she drew a deep breath. It was better now. Her pulse was slowing, and her heartbeat had quieted.

Her breathing was shallow but regular. And the buzzing in her ears had receded, replaced by the noise of the party: tinkling ice, laughter, conversations shouted above a local rock combo.

Teddi shook her head and passed a hand over her eyes. Seeing the snow and feeling the cold was a shock to her system, one she supposed she would become accustomed to, but not immediately. Maybe she was expecting too much of herself too soon. After all, she'd only arrived at her parents' Vail lodge this morning.

"Teddi? Is that you?"

She might have guessed that she couldn't hide in this alcove forever. Smothering a sigh, Teddi straightened and pasted a smile on her lips, then relaxed with genuine pleasure when she recognized Kelly Martin.

"You look wonderful," Teddi said, returning Kelly's enthusiastic embrace. "Having babies agrees with you."

Kelly laughed. "Liar." Her dark eyes twinkled. "I'm fifteen pounds heavier than I was the last time I saw you. And believe me, diapers and night feedings don't agree with anyone." Tilting her head, she examined Teddi, then heaved a sigh of mock despair. "You look gorgeous. Now I remember why I hated you in high school and envied you in college."

Teddi grinned. "Now who's the liar? Remember that Sigma Chi? Eric Somebody? You stole him from under my nose."

"One of the high points of my life." Holding hands, they smiled at each other. "It's good to see you, Teddi. You could write something more than a scribbled Christmas card, you know. How are you—really?"

"I'm fine—really." Even standing in the alcove away from the combo near the lodge door and the main thrust of her parents' anniversary party, they had to shout to be heard. "I love my job, love Lahaina. Things couldn't be better."

If that were true, then why did she occasionally experience a vague restlessness, as if something were missing? A fleeting expression of annoyance darkened Teddi's blue eyes. This was hardly the moment for self-examination.

Kelly pressed her hands. "I'm glad you came home to help Hans and Marta celebrate. It wouldn't have been right without you."

"What? I can't hear."

"... talk about you all the time. I know it means the world to them that ..."

A flush of discomfort tinged Teddi's cheeks. It wasn't as if she hadn't seen her parents; they'd visited her in Lahaina. But she knew the trip was long and arduous at their age, and expensive. It would have been easier if Teddi had flown to Colorado as she had this time.

Teddi turned away from Kelly's curious gaze. Well, she was here now. And it was every bit as upsetting as she'd imagined it would be. Memory assaulted her at every turn, and she wasn't convinced that she'd ever again be entirely comfortable with snow and cold.

Searching the large room, she found her parents standing before the registration counter, accepting congratulations. They were beaming with pleasure and pride, holding hands and looking younger than white hair and creased faces would indicate. Still, it shocked Teddi to realize how they had aged in the past six years. She wished with all her heart that she could give them the one thing they most wanted— herself. But she couldn't.

Smiling, Marta blew a kiss toward the alcove, and Hans waved, gesturing her into the crush of guests, some of whom Teddi knew, most of whom she did not.

Teddi nodded and mouthed, "In a minute." Then a man strode through the door, bringing with him a swirl of snowflakes. "Who is that?" she asked, staring.

Kelly grinned. "Isn't he a hunk?"

"Outstanding," Teddi agreed. She and Kelly weren't the only women whose heads turned toward the tall man pulling his ski cap from tousled russet hair. Teddi smiled as she noticed half a dozen predatory females itching to run over and help him with his scarf and coat. She imagined he was used to it.

He was tall, six feet three at least, wearing a black-and-red ski sweater over black ski pants. Unlike most of the men in the lodge, Teddi knew immediately this man wasn't just a weekend skier. A lean, muscled body, told her he was a serious athlete. And he hadn't gotten that deep bronzed tan by sitting under a sunlamp—it was the real thing.

Watching as he kissed her mother's cheek and gripped her father's hand, Teddi decided he had what she termed "too good to be true" looks. He moved with a fluid grace and an erect posture that announced an unshakable confidence. A chiseled nose offset a craggy outdoor face, and thick dark brows framed warm brown eyes. When he bent near her mother's ear, his curly brown hair glinted red beneath the lights, and a wide smile illuminated his features.

"Who is he?" Teddi asked curiously. If Kelly had revealed he was a movie star or a male model, Teddi wouldn't have been surprised. He possessed a presence that suggested he was accustomed to public attention.

"Grant Sterling," Kelly shouted in her ear. "He took the silver medal in cross-country skiing at

Lake Placid in 1980. He owns the Sterling ski shops—equipment and apparel.''

Teddi's mouth dropped. *That* was Grant Sterling? He wasn't at all what she'd envisioned from her parents' letters. For some reason she'd expected blond, medium size and boyish, maybe thick-lensed glasses. She'd been steeling herself for someone vaguely resembling her brother, Peter. Instead, Grant Sterling was tall, dark and anything but boyish. Teddi knew he was the same age as Peter would have been, two years older than her own twenty-six. But his handsomely weathered face suggested a maturity beyond his years, something Teddi hadn't anticipated.

"He's a catch," Kelly went on cheerfully. "He's handsome, charming, owns a gorgeous home, and besides the ski shop downstairs, he has them in Aspen and Denver, too.''

"I know.'' Teddi responded absently. She doubted there was much about Grant Sterling that she didn't know. Sooner or later everything he did appeared in her parents' letters. Frankly, it concerned her. It was just possible that Marta and Hans were making a surrogate son of Grant Sterling. This worry was the primary reason Teddi had caved in and decided to fly home. She understood her parents' need, but she didn't understand why Grant Sterling seemed so willing to fill it. She meant to find out.

"Come on," Kelly said, "I'll introduce you. I'd forgotten you don't know Grant. He moved to Vail the year after—" She bit her lip and halted abruptly. An anxious frown drew her brows. "Sorry," she muttered softly.

"It's okay," Teddi said easily. But she heard the strain in her tone that said it was not okay. She mustered a smile. "I expect Mr. Sterling and I will meet soon enough."

"Look, Teddi . . ."

"Really, Kelly, it's okay. Honest." But it wasn't. Teddi felt her heart thud against her rib cage, rubbed clammy palms over her ski pants. Her teeth clamped. She'd known this would happen; she'd dreaded it.

Kelly rose on tiptoes and waved at a man in the crowd, then shouted, "I'm coming." She shrugged apologetically. "I promised Jim we'd leave early. The baby has a cold." After hugging Teddi, she squeezed her hands. "Let's have a long catch-up lunch next week, all right?"

"I'd like that."

"Good. I'll call you."

Delaying the inevitable, Teddi approached a table overflowing with canapés and finger food. She chose a pinwheel of ham and cream cheese, pretending she wanted it, and wandered away from the group near the center of the table.

She had to pull herself together. Tossing a wave of silky blond hair over her shoulder, Teddi stared at nothing and decided she should have flown in a few days earlier. It might have given her time to come to terms with the past, if that was possible, before meeting her parents' friends and seeing her own friends again. As it was, she wasn't handling the situation with her usual confidence and ease.

Tilting her head, Teddi stared at the staircase leading up to the balcony that opened onto the family's quarters. As did everything else, it reminded her of Peter. She and Peter had played on those stairs years before they were carpeted. They had sailed paper airplanes from the balcony.

A deep baritone cut across her thoughts. "Are you all right?"

Teddi blinked at the ham-and-cheese pinwheel posed midway to her mouth. Then she raised her head and stared into Grant Sterling's curious gaze.

"Yes, I . . ." It embarrassed her to be caught in a moment of vulnerability. "I'm fine."

He smiled down at her. "You look like you were a million miles away."

She had been. She'd been lost in another time, watching ghosts. Peter . . . and Kip. A line of knots tensed her jawline.

Teddi drew a long, slow breath, then extended her hand. "I'm Teddi Ansel, Hans and Marta's daughter."

"I know." A firm warm hand enclosed hers. "I'm Grant Sterling."

"I know."

What she hadn't known or previously noticed was that he carried a cane. Automatically, her gaze swept his feet, looking for the cast that was by no means unusual in a ski resort. There was none. And she didn't recall seeing a limp.

Teddi released a sigh. On Maui the phonies wore designer sunglasses for effect or carried surfboards that seldom rode a wave. This was only the second time she'd seen someone flaunting a cane. Affectations annoyed her, though she admitted Grant Sterling at least possessed the confidence and polish to carry it off.

"I want to thank you for all the help you've been to my parents," she said smoothly, hoping none of her thoughts appeared in her expression. Whatever else he might be, Grant Sterling had been a great help at the lodge. According to her parents, there had been times when they couldn't have managed without him. Teddi didn't relish this fact, but she couldn't ignore it, either.

"I'm glad to help out when I can," he said. "Hans and Marta have told me a lot about you." He reached past her to fill a plate with ham slices and cheese. Straightening, he smiled down into her eyes. "When they told me how beautiful you were,

I thought it was simply parents' pride speaking. But you really are breathtaking.''

Spoken so simply, the compliment sounded like a statement of fact rather than the idle flattery Teddi suspected it really was. Grant Sterling had clearly charmed her parents, but she didn't intend to be so easy a conquest. She'd made up her mind about him the moment she saw the cane. And no cast or limp.

Her smile was pleasant but cool. "I think I'd rather be complimented for my accomplishments than for how I wear my hair or how skilled I may be at applying makeup," she said lightly.

Grant's thick eyebrows arched, and amusement twinkled in his eyes. "Then let's try again. Congratulations on your promotion. I understand you've been appointed executive administrator for the Royal Alii."

Teddi darted an uneasy look toward her parents, wondering what else Grant Sterling knew about her. "Thank you," she murmured with a graciousness she didn't really feel.

"What exactly is an executive administrator?"

The way he leaned on the cane reminded Teddi of a pose from an English drawing-room stage play. She almost rolled her eyes and said, "Oh, brother!" And she wondered how many times he'd rehearsed to perfect the gesture, to make it seem natural and unplanned. Stifling an impulse to applaud, she grudgingly conceded he did it well.

"An executive administrator is . . ." She waved a hand, searching for an adequate explanation. "Someone above a manager but lacking the authority of an owner." Close enough.

"What does an executive administrator do?"

Teddi watched his strong white teeth bite into the ham and cheese and decided this was a ridiculous conversation. He couldn't possibly care what she did every day. And she didn't relish shouting her schedule into his ear. Stepping backward, she eased away from the provocative scent of his musky aftershave. "A little of everything," she responded vaguely.

Nodding, he hooked the cane over his arm and finished the sandwich, his gaze sliding over her silky blond hair, her well-filled sweater and the blue ski pants molding her hips.

The directness of his admiration brought a flash of annoyance to Teddi's eyes. Although she was accustomed to dealing with men's stares, most had the grace to be discreet. That she was blushing and experiencing a surprising stir of response angered her. She intended to approach Grant Sterling warily, maintaining a distance until she knew more about him. Much more.

"I'd like to know you better, Teddi Ansel."

"Why is that, Mr. Sterling?"

"Mr. Sterling?" His rich, full laughter invited listeners to join. "Well, first, you're a beautiful woman. Second, you're Hans and Marta's daughter. And third, I think we have a lot in common."

"Oh?"

After placing his plate on the table, he leaned on his cane and smiled at her. "Do you play bridge?"

"No," she said, secretly pleased that he'd guessed wrong. "I hate card games. Sorry."

"I hate card games, too. Never learned to play bridge. Do you enjoy chess?"

Teddi frowned. "I play, but it's not a favorite. I like things that move fast."

"So do I. Chess puts me to sleep. How about jazz?"

"It sounds like noise to me."

"Me, too. Watch much TV?"

"I'd rather read a good book."

"Same here." The red-and-black ski sweater lifted around a shrug, and his mouth widened in an engaging grin. "There you have it. We hate the same things. Obviously we're made for each other."

Teddi stared, then burst into laughter. He'd taken her by surprise. A wave of golden hair flowed over her shoulder as she cocked her head. She had to admit he certainly wasn't lacking in the charm department. "Ah, but do we *like* the same things?"

Good heavens. Was it this easy to fall under his spell? Immediately, she straightened, the mischievous glint fading from her eyes. She wished she could withdraw the question.

"Well, let's see." Grant narrowed one eye and regarded her speculatively. "You're crazy about country and classical music—right?"

"Right," Teddi agreed reluctantly. Was there anything her parents hadn't told him?

"And naturally you love sports. Swimming, tennis, golf, the works."

"And you do, too," she said.

"I don't play tennis, but just about everything else."

Teddi met his smile. "Yes, tennis would be difficult." Her eyes flicked to the cane. She had intended a hint of sarcasm, but he didn't seem to notice.

"Right," he answered cheerfully. Leaning on the cane, he contemplated her for a moment. "May I ask you something?"

Teddi smiled. "Is there anything left that my parents haven't already told you?"

Curiosity deepened the tawny flecks in his eyes. "Why did you drop out? Everyone thought you'd take the gold in women's downhill."

Teddi's hands jerked, and the blood drained from her face. An icy wave began at her toes and rushed upward. He'd struck out at her—and hard.

She wet her lips, feeling the tremble beneath her tongue. "If you'll excuse me, my parents are waving..."

The touch of his hand on her arm made her jump. She stared at his fingers, feeling an electric warmth penetrate her sudden chill.

"Is something wrong?"

"I think you know what's wrong," she whispered. Her voice seemed to have disappeared.

"Teddi, will you ski with me tomorrow?"

"No!" After drawing a quick breath and pulling from his hand, she softened the rejection with a lie. "I have other plans."

"Lunch, then? At the Ore House?"

With a shock, Teddi realized she was unconsciously leaning toward him. Her dislike hadn't filtered through to her traitorous body. Squaring her shoulders, she clasped her hands in front of her as a fleeting confusion raced along her nerves. She absolutely did not want to respond to Grant Sterling. But when she looked into his eyes, brown with a tawny hint of gold flecks, her breath caught in her throat. It was idiotic, a betrayal.

Logic blocked her urge to refuse his invitation. How could she discover his relationship with her parents if she didn't talk to him?

"All right," she conceded, frowning. "Lunch tomorrow."

He called to her before she pressed into the crowd. "Teddi? I'm glad you decided to come home. It means more than you know to Hans and Marta."

But not more than *he* knew? Teddi stared at him over her shoulder, anger tightening her lips. He possessed a colossal arrogance. But then, what skier didn't? They had to possess arrogance to believe they could beat the mountain. Hadn't Kip and Peter said so? And she, as well? Oh, God. Now she was doing it. Tearing at scars, discovering afresh how raw the wounds still were.

Tossing back her hair with an irritated motion, Teddi pushed blindly through the crowd, smiling and nodding automatically. Her breathing didn't calm until she stood beside her parents, relaxing in their familiar presence, silently drawing on their solid strength.

Marta's soft hand squeezed hers. Her eyes glowed. "It's a lovely party, isn't it? So many friends."

"Happy anniversary." Teddi kissed her mother's cheek and reached to press her father's hand. A flow of people passed before her.

"Theodora! You're home!"

Teddi shook Bill Haverford's hand and kissed Grace's temple. And prepared herself to hear the standard story.

Bill winked a twinkling eye. "Do you remember stealing licorice from my store?"

Teddi smiled despite the tired familiarity of the question. They had replayed this scene so often over the years that Teddi knew she could recite the dialogue by heart. But Bill Haverford was a good friend to her parents. "I don't recall the grand theft, but I remember the consequences. Dad hauled me down to the Jelly Bean and made me return the ill-gotten goods. That was the most humiliating day of my life."

"Hans and I planned it. I was supposed to threaten you with jail, but I couldn't do it. You had those pigtails, and the biggest, wettest blue eyes..."

Teddi spoke the obligatory response. "You terrified me. I haven't so much as cheated on my tax returns since."

Bill patted her cheek fondly. "We had to do it, Theodora. It was a hard lesson but a good one. Right, Hans?"

Teddi's father smiled at her, paternal pride lighting his bright eyes. "She's a good girl, my Theodora."

Like Marta, Hans Ansel spoke with an accent that had diminished over the years but had not vanished, as he and Marta stubbornly insisted. They always expressed surprise when a guest asked where they were from. As they'd now spent more years in the United States than they had in Switzerland, they always answered proudly that they were American, pointing to the framed citizenship papers prominently hung behind the counter.

What they had accomplished through hard work, self-denial and sheer determination made Teddi proud to be their daughter. She wished Peter could have been here tonight to see the room crowded with friends and well-wishers. For a moment her eyes held her mother's, and she knew they were sharing the same thought.

"No sadness, Theodora," Marta whispered. "Not tonight."

More to please her parents than herself, Teddi summoned a gaiety she didn't feel and eased into the festivities. Placing a distance between herself and Grant Sterling, she mingled with the guests, greeting old friends, meeting friends her parents had made in her absence.

After Hans and Marta had cut the anniversary cake and been toasted with champagne while they opened a mound of gifts, the combo settled into slower music, more suitable for intimate dancing.

"May I?" A hand lightly touched her hair, and Teddi turned to look into Grant's warm eyes.

Hesitating, Teddi remembered her uncharacteristic response when Grant had simply touched her arm. On the other hand, she didn't want him to think she was afraid of him. Her full lips curved into an indifferent smile. "If you like," she agreed politely.

She stepped into his arms as the combo swung into their twentieth rendition of "Edelweiss" in honor of the inn's name. Deliberately, she opened a wide space between herself and her partner.

Instead of moving forward immediately, he held her for a long moment before he grinned down at her, then firmly guided her against the long, hard length of his body.

"I can't lead unless I can feel you."

Arching an eyebrow, Teddi asked sweetly, "Do many women believe that?" But to her disgust, her rebellious body didn't move back. She fit into his arms as if she belonged there.

His breath stirred the golden tendrils at her temple. He held her in a firm embrace, his large hand spreading an aura of warmth over her back, the muscles tensing in his thighs. An explosion of heat erupted through Teddi's body as she inhaled the minty scent of his breath, the disturbing musky fragrance of his after-shave.

She told herself the dance would be over in a few fleeting minutes, and she held on to that thought as a defense against the uncomfortable sensations coursing through her mind and body. Warmth, strength. She was acutely conscious of her breasts brushing his wide chest, of his hard thighs leading her into a slow turn. And each accidental touch shot an electric jolt through her nervous system.

This was crazy. She was actually wondering how his kiss would taste. Sheer insanity. She didn't know him, and she didn't want to. So why couldn't her rebellious body accept that?

Inhaling deeply, she tried to concentrate on the music. Instead, Grant's after-shave teased her senses. She felt his arms strong and protective around her, felt his warmth enclosing her hand and burning through the back of her sweater. His body pressed possessively against hers; his warm breath stirred her hair; his lips rested intimately against her temple. Closing her eyes, Teddi stumbled and swallowed hard.

In Maui, keeping her emotions in check presented no difficulty. But returning home had triggered an awakening. Her emotions were running amok. And it didn't require much introspection to realize Grant Sterling was the catalyst. Something about him demolished her carefully erected defenses. That he'd managed to reach her on a raw physical level so quickly and so effortlessly astonished her.

Relief flooded Teddi's features when the music ended.

"Was it that bad?" Grant smiled. "Did I mangle your toes?" He lifted the cane from the back of a chair and leaned on it. Although he continued to smile, his eyes reflected a dark intensity that indicated he was as aware of Teddi as she was of him.

"No," Teddi answered as the combo blasted through "Good Night, Ladies" and the remaining guests began to drift toward the door. She glanced at the grandfather clock her parents had brought with them from Switzerland. "I didn't realize it was almost two."

"Tired?" His hand rose to stroke her cheek; the gentle, almost-tentative, contact of his palm on her overheated face seemed to paralyze her. "Are you sure you won't join me on the slopes?"

"I'm very sure," Teddi snapped, irritated by her response to his touch. Her chest felt tight, and her cheek flamed where he'd brushed it. To her bewilderment, she found herself walking beside him toward the coatracks. Making an effort to lighten her tone, she asked, "How do you find time to ski? Don't you have to work? Or do the Sterling ski shops manage themselves?"

"At this point, they pretty much manage themselves." He shrugged into an expensive parka and settled his cap over russet curls. A wide grin flashed teeth that appeared impossibly white against his tan. "Besides, I have a very capable executive administrator."

Teddi's eyes narrowed, and she spoke around a tight smile. "You're an annoying man, Mr. Sterling."

"But lovable, Ms Ansel. A staunch supporter of God, motherhood and apple pie. I have good qualities you don't even suspect."

Teddi nodded slowly. "That remains to be seen."

His twinkling gaze swept her lips. "I certainly hope so." Then he opened the door, gave her a jaunty salute and stepped into the blowing snow.

Chapter Two

Teddi's usual work attire was a brightly colored muumuu or a crisp linen suit. The balance of her wardrobe was a collection of swim- and sportswear. She wouldn't have owned anything suitable for snow and cold if Marta hadn't kept her room exactly as it had been when she'd left—including a closetful of clothing.

After slipping out of the Levi's she'd worn to help clean up the party debris from the night before, Teddi pulled the scarf from her head and shook out her hair, contemplating the contents of her closet.

Eventually she chose navy ski pants and a Norwegian cable-knit sweater. Thankfully, ski fashions didn't change much; otherwise, she would have been hopelessly out of style. But other than an additional fullness in the breast, her clothes still fit well, which pleased her.

It didn't please her, however, to be wearing ski clothes at all, but that couldn't be helped. Teddi brushed her hair into a shining knot atop her head, then tugged on a red ski cap. She was as ready as she was going to be for her lunch with Grant. Which meant she didn't feel ready at all.

Crossing to her window, she looped back the drapes and raised the blind, blinking at the sun-sharp glare bouncing off the snow. It was a splendid day—if one admired fresh, untrampled snow and thirty-five-degree weather. Sighing, Teddi lifted her gaze to a clear Colorado sky so blue she wouldn't have believed the color had she observed it in a painting.

This was the type of brisk, cold day she'd loved as a child. For an instant the clock swung backward, and Teddi was twelve again, peering at the Gore Range with excitement sparkling in her eyes, eager to step into her skis and fly down the mountain. Deep powder would have filled the back bowls after last night's snow and was sprinkled over the north face like a sugary invitation. Smiling, Teddi could almost hear Peter calling from the next room, "Hurry up, squirt. We're late. The coach will be mad."

Shaking time's echo from her thoughts, Teddi whirled from the window, but there was no escape from the past. Her room was a storehouse of memories.

The wall over the brass bed showcased a dozen years of trophies and ribbons. Tiny gold figurines, perched atop wooden bases, gleamed in the morning light. The ribbons were faded now, but once they had been as bold and proud as Teddi herself. Or so people had said. She stared at the shelves and corkboard, trying to recall the girl who had won all those meets. Where had she gone?

To Maui. To a land, a climate and a life as far removed from what she had known as she could get.

Part of Teddi's thoughts mourned the loss of innocence and opportunity. Another part shrank from evidence of a life she bitterly rejected. Pushing abruptly from the window, she made a vow to box every trophy and ribbon, every yellowing clipping, and carry them to the darkest corner of the storeroom. And the photographs, too. Especially the photographs.

Reaching a trembling finger, she lightly stroked the frame atop her bureau. Beneath the glass, Peter's arm circled her shoulders, Kip's hand rested possessively on her waist. They stood before a fence they'd made by thrusting their skis in the snow, and they were grinning crazily, making victory signs with their mittened fingers.

Teddi bit her lip. She remembered that day as if it were yesterday—it had been the day dreams came true. That morning they had learned that all three had qualified for the Olympic team. Later that night, Kip had slid an engagement ring on her finger. They'd been young and healthy and blissfully happy and oh, so innocent. They had believed the mountain was theirs, that nothing could stop them. They had believed in themselves and in each other.

They had believed they had forever.

Teddi slammed the photograph facedown on the bureau hard enough to crack the glass. Sinking to the bed, she covered her face with shaking hands.

"I'm sorry," she whispered hoarsely.

Sorry for what? Sorry that she was alive? Sorry that she had survived and Peter and Kip had not?

Oh, Lord, why had she done this to herself? Why had she come back here, to this? Why hadn't she stayed in Maui where she was free from torturous thoughts and self-recrimination? She hadn't tormented herself like this in years.

Jumping up, she dashed from the room and slammed the door firmly behind her. And she wouldn't allow herself to glance at Peter's closed door as she rushed toward the balcony. It was like her own room, crowded with bits and pieces of his life, a room Marta and Hans could slip into when memory needed nudging.

At the balcony, Teddi paused and leaned on the railing, willing herself back to the present by viewing the scene below through professional eyes. Years of experience plus a degree in hotel-and-restaurant management qualified her to assess the business at a glance.

She watched as her mother pushed the register across the counter toward a young couple with luggage and skis piled at their feet. Her father was probably in the restaurant overseeing the preparation of his specialty, Wiener schnitzel, for the lunch crowd. A sad-eyed young man was sprawled across a sofa, his cast thrust out for a ring of admirers to sign. Two dark-haired women emerged from the staircase leading to the expensive shops on the lower level. Teddi wondered if any of the packages they carried came from the Sterling ski shop.

Automatically, her eyes flicked to the grandfather clock near the dining-room door. If she didn't hurry, she'd miss the shuttle into the village. Taking the shuttle was an inconvenience at times, Teddi thought, but in Vail no one traveled by car; the main village was barred to private vehicles.

After snatching up a parka, Teddi ran lightly down the stairs and waited while her mother called for the bell captain and explained to the young couple that their room was located in the new wing. When they'd departed, Marta kissed Teddi's cheek and smiled.

"I'm glad you're making an effort to know Grant. He's been a big help to us. And he's a lot like Peter, don't you think?"

So far, Teddi hadn't noticed anything about Grant Sterling that reminded her of Peter. Peter had been genuine and open, not prone to surface charm or affectations. "Maybe," she hedged, not wanting to offend her mother's feelings for Grant. "Sure you don't need me here?"

"This is your vacation, remember?" Marta waved her toward the door. "If you enjoy yourself, maybe you'll come home again soon." Immediately, a sheepish smile pleated the wrinkles folding her cheeks. "I swore I wouldn't say anything like that."

"I'm having a wonderful time," Teddi lied brightly, wrapping her mother in a hug. But silently she had been ticking off the days—three down, eleven to go. Then she could stop pretending and return to Maui.

"Good." Marta upended the key bucket behind the counter, spilling keyes out for sorting. "Oh, would you ask Grant to order more firewood? I think we're running low again."

A tiny alarm sounded in Teddi's mind. "No need to bother Mr. Sterling," she said, pulling on her gloves. "I'll take care of it when I return. It'll make me feel useful."

"But Grant always—"

"Gotta run or I'll miss the shuttle. See you later."

TEDDI WAS RELIEVED to discover she'd arrived before Grant. She suspected he would have requested an outside table, as she would have done once upon a time. Firmly, she told the waiter she preferred a table inside.

After ordering a drink, Teddi tried to relax and thought about her mother's request.

She simply couldn't visualize her parents being dependent on anyone but themselves. The idea was not only ludicrous but also repugnant. It wasn't like them.

Hans had built the original inn himself, and Marta had sewn the curtains and quilted the bedspreads. They had been too proud to accept help. And they'd made the move from Bern to Vail, from shopkeeper to innkeeper, at an age when most people were considering retirement.

"A penny for your thoughts?" Grant dropped into the chair facing her after removing his parka and hooking his cane over a chair rung. He ordered a drink from the waiter, who arrived at their table simultaneously, then smiled at Teddi.

"Nothing earthshaking," she responded thinly.

"Try me." His habit of gazing directly into a person's eyes was disconcerting.

"I was thinking about my parents. How they always had the courage to do things later than most people. They didn't marry until they were in their thirties; Mom was forty when Peter was born, forty-two when I arrived; they were almost fifty when they made their permanent move to the United States and built the Edelweiss.'' She paused while the waiter placed a hot buttered rum before Grant and offered her a refill. ''I warned you— pretty dull stuff to anyone outside the family.''

''Not at all.'' Smiling, he raised his tankard to hers. ''Here's to the Ansels and Vail's early days. I wish I'd been here then.''

Teddi laughed. ''Bite your tongue. When we arrived in the mid-sixties, there was no TV and only dubious radio reception. The nearest movie theater was six miles away in Minturn—and the movies were shown on two bed sheets sewn together. It was pretty primitive. I was entering junior high before we had a permanent location for the school. In those days, no one could predict if Vail would succeed.''

Grant's dark eyes swept the crowded restaurant, and a lopsided grin lit his features. ''I think it's going to make it.''

''I think you're right.'' She didn't want to wander too far from the subject. ''And my parents helped it happen.''

''They're fine people, Teddi. Very special. I don't think Hans and Marta ever met a stranger. I'm very fond of them.''

''They're fond of you, too.'' She drew a breath and met his eyes. ''Perhaps too fond.''

He frowned over the rim of his tankard. "What does that mean?"

The waiter's interruption staved off an immediate reply. Teddi ordered the first thing she saw on the menu. Pita bread stuffed with something. It really didn't matter; there was no way she could enjoy this lunch. When the waiter drifted away, she clasped her hands and leaned forward. "Grant, my parents are almost seventy."

"What does their age have to do with anything?"

Frowning, Teddi sensed she wasn't handling this well. She was skirting the issue, looking for a tactful approach where none existed.

"At their age it's difficult to bounce back. They're vulnerable right now," she said slowly, feeling her way. "I don't think they've recovered from Peter's death. It was a devastating shock." The words sounded so mundane, so painfully ordinary. They didn't begin to convey the impact of Peter's loss. "Look, it would be very easy for my parents to transer their affection to the first available person who—"

Grant raised a hand. "Wait a minute. I think I see where this is leading. Are you suggesting that I've taken Peter's place?"

"You tell me."

"No one is going to replace Peter, Teddi. And I don't agree that Hans and Marta are walking wounded. Not for that reason, not after five years. Yes, they've kept Peter's room intact." He gave her a steady, level look. "But yours is intact, also. I don't think it means anything darkly significant."

She stared at him, at the tiny crinkles fanning out from the corners of his eyes, at the russet curls against his tanned skin. He had the kind of face better suited for a mountain man, or maybe a pirate. And he possessed that type of unassailable strength. She had felt it when they danced, and she read it now in his unwavering gaze.

"Being an outsider," she said pointedly, "you couldn't possibly understand the depth of our loss."

Watching her, Grant leaned back as the waiter set platters before them. His golden-brown eyes were sober and thoughtful. "Just for the sake of argument, let's assume for a moment that you're right— Hans and Marta look at me as a replacement for Peter. Is that so terrible?"

"What are you saying?" She glanced at the bean sprouts spilling from the pita bread with a grimace of distaste. She couldn't have swallowed a bite.

Grant shrugged. "As you pointed out, your parents are old. Frankly, they can use some help. If Peter were alive, he'd provide that help. As it is . . . they have no son, and I have no parents." He spread his hands. "Maybe we need each other. Where's the harm?"

Teddi felt like a fool. Her shoulders slumped, and she waved a limp hand. "I didn't know…about your parents. What happened to them?" Then, embarrassed by her boldness, she said, "I'm sorry, I have no right—"

The touch of his warm fingers as they covered her hand startled her. "It's all right. My mother was a frightened sixteen-year-old who thought giving up her baby was the right thing to do. And maybe it was. For her."

"You found her?" Teddi didn't know what else to say.

He nodded. "I found a frightened forty-year-old who didn't want the past intruding on her current life."

Teddi released a long breath and looked at him. "Look, Grant, I think I owe you an apology. I was so worried about my parents here alone, I thought—"

"There's no need." His warm caramel eyes smiled. "I can understand your concern. Some guy appears from nowhere and adopts your parents—in your place I'd be concerned, too."

"I just don't want them hurt."

He leaned back in his chair and studied her. "I love Hans and Marta, Teddi. I can assure you they aren't going to be hurt by me."

Frowning, Teddi poked at the pita bread for a moment, then gave it up and pushed the platter aside. Something in his voice struck her wrong. An odd emphasis—something. It almost sounded like an accusation.

The problem was, she couldn't be sure. It was increasingly difficult to focus on the topic at hand. When Grant spoke, Teddi discovered herself responding to his rich baritone rather than to his words. Her eyes seemed drawn to his mouth, and she was confusingly fascinated by his hands, large square hands that tapered to strong capable fingers.

Irritation pinched her lips. This wasn't like her. She didn't fall apart when a man looked at her. Or smiled or brushed her hand with strong tanned fingers. She put them in their place. And their place lay firmly outside her emotional range. That's how she wanted it. No involvements, no heart-wrenching relationships. Never again.

And that's how it had been. Until now. Somehow Grant Sterling had managed to slip past her resolve. Otherwise, she wouldn't feel so stupidly fluttery inside when those tawny eyes met hers.

She drained the last drops of her buttered rum, then moved the tankard across the cloth in small wet circles. "Thanks for explaining. I feel better."

His stare sent a rush of heat spiraling up from her toes. "Hans and Marta need *someone*, Teddi."

This time there was no mistaking the emphasis. Teddi straightened in her chair and forgot the strange tension his nearness caused. "I'm not sure I like your tone."

A hint of anger heightened the gold in his dark eyes. "We've talked about me; now let's talk about you. Hans and Marta are considering retirement. I think you know they'd like you to take over the Edelweiss. Their greatest fear is that years of hard work and high hopes will pass to a stranger. So why are you resisting? Why aren't you in Vail permanently, Teddi?"

A rush of anger heated her face. "That's family business," she snapped. "And none of yours. But since you seem to think it is, perhaps you'd like to know that I don't want the Edelweiss. I have a fantastic job in an area I love. I'm satisfied and happy with my life exactly as it is. I don't want to move back here. Has that occurred to you?"

"Yes. And I rejected the thought as being too damned selfish to be worthy of a daughter of Hans and Marta."

Teddi gasped. Her mouth dropped open, then snapped shut, and her blue eyes blazed as she leaned toward him. "How dare you!" she whispered through gritted teeth. "Who the hell are you to pass judgment on me?"

"Someone who's worried about your parents, Teddi. Someone who doesn't understand your reasoning but would like to." Their eyes clashed across the table. "I'm here doing the things you should be doing because apparently you either don't care enough to help out or you just can't be bothered."

Teddi stiffened with shock. "I don't have to listen to this."

"Tell me again how you don't want them hurt, Teddi. Then look into their eyes."

Her hands were shaking so badly that she couldn't get the napkin off her lap and onto the table.

Grant watched her struggle to rise. "We can talk about this, or you can run away like you've done in the past."

The color drained from Teddi's cheeks at his audacity. No one had ever spoken to her like this.

"Have you ever once considered what happened from your parents' point of view?" Grant continued. "They didn't lose just Peter—they lost *both* their children. Peter died and you ran away."

"Stop it!" she hissed. Scarlet flamed on her cheeks; her mouth trembled uncontrollably. For the first time in her life she wanted to physically strike another human being.

He hooked an arm over the top of the chair and stared at her. "If I'm wrong, tell me."

She was standing now, experiencing a strangling fury that would have rendered any attempt at conversation incoherent. Snatching up her parka and gloves, Teddi struggled to find the control needed to leave the restaurant.

"I don't owe you any explanations," she sputtered. She wanted to say more, but there was no point. Spinning, she rushed toward the door.

She'd reached the shuttle stop before she saw him emerge from the Ore House. An icy wind bathed the anger heating her cheeks, and inside her pockets her hands clenched into fists. It provided scant satisfaction to notice Grant was as upset as she. His thick brows were knit so tightly they looked like a straight slash across his forehead. His mouth was hard and set. And he was limping as he followed her, using the cane to support his right leg.

Teddi made a small sound of disgust. Was she supposed to think he'd injured himself on the slopes this morning? Or maybe he was trying to convince her to feel sorry for him. Well, it was too late. He'd forgotten that she'd danced with him. And he couldn't have managed a fox-trot on a sprained ankle.

Dashing forward, she jumped aboard the shuttle, silently willing the driver to pull from the curb before Grant reached them. He'd outfoxed himself by pretending to limp, she realized with a grim smile. Either he had to abandon the limp or miss the shuttle. From the corner of her eye, Teddi watched him hobble toward the back of the shuttle and raise his cane to knock on the window.

And her grin widened as the oblivious driver shifted and lurched forward. The cane tapped thin air. And Mr. Grant Sterling damned near fell flat on his handsome face. She twisted in the seat to see him waving his arms, slipping and sliding on the ice. To her immense disappointment, he didn't fall.

She was still seething when she stamped the snow from her boots on the Edelweiss's wide veranda. Teddi hurried through the main lodge, raising a hand to her mother, who smiled from behind the registration counter. But halfway up the balcony steps, Teddi halted. Where was she going? Her bedroom was no refuge.

Spinning in an about-face, she retraced her steps. An urge to *do* something pumped adrenaline through her system. In days past, she would have grabbed up her skis and vented her frustrations on the mountain. But that was unthinkable now.

Throwing aside her parka and cap, Teddi shook back her hair and strode to the baby grand near the veranda windows. She flexed her fingers and wondered if she could still play after so many years without practice.

First she rummaged through the music books, searching for an easy piece while she limbered her fingers across the keys. Marta looked up and smiled encouragement, and Hans poked his head out of the dining room and waved happily.

Rachmaninoff emerged without much difficulty, but the sweetness and romance grated against her mood. Grant's "too good to be true" face floated in front of the keys. Frowning, Teddi lifted her fingers and flipped through the music sheets.

Bach and Beethoven rolled over the lodge, and then Wagner. The heavy crashing music expressed her anger and satisfied it. And gradually, gradually, the tension drained away.

GRANT STERLING pulled up beside the registration desk, listening to the music, watching Teddi's fingers fly over the keys. She displayed the same intensity, the same tightly focused concentration, that had made her a fine skier.

He'd been in the crowd that had watched Teddi's qualifying run, the run that had secured her position on the Olympic team. Though he'd observed other runs before and since, hers possessed a quality that had made it unforgettable.

She'd worn powder blue, he remembered, and a blue-and-red cap. She'd looked small and vulnerable standing alone at the starting gate, staring down at the snow and flags and the crowd waiting at the bottom of the run. Grant had shaded his eyes and looked up at her, knowing what she was feeling as he'd completed his own qualifying trek two days earlier. Anxiety, determination, and most of all, hope. Hope that all the years of hard work were about to reach fruition, hope that she wouldn't disappoint her family, her coach and the team.

Hope, deep and consuming, that she would have a chance at the gold.

Then she had seated her goggles, gripped her poles and pushed off. He remembered drawing a sharp breath as she flew between the flags, remembered thinking he had never seen anyone so graceful. Like all gifted athletes, Teddi Ansel had made it look easy, had made speeding down the mountain seem natural and effortless. When she cut to a glide at the bottom, there had been a moment of awed silence, then wild applause. And he'd seen by her face that she knew she'd made it. They had all known it that day. She was simply the best.

"What a tragedy," he murmured, watching her bend to Wagner. "What a damned waste."

Marta laid her hand on his arm. "She would have won."

Together they watched Teddi losing herself in the music. "Everyone in America thought so," Grant said. Then he covered Marta's veined hand with his own and smiled into her eyes. "How are you feeling today?"

"Fine, never felt better. After all, my daughter's home." She tilted an eyebrow and gave him a stern look. "Remember—you promised. Not a word to her."

"I really think—"

Marta placed a finger across his lips, then gave him a gentle push toward the phone. "We need firewood. Will you call your friend, the one who gives the discount, and order three cords?"

As he dialed the number, his eyes strayed to Teddi. He'd been hard on her at lunch, had said things he wouldn't have said had he not been so fond of Hans and Marta. And if he hadn't known how much they missed her, how much they needed her.

The discordant music filling the lodge told him how deeply he'd wounded her, and he regretted the necessity. Teddi had been partially correct regarding his relationship with Hans and Marta; in many respects, he had adopted them. But the bottom line was that he wasn't part of their family and Teddi was. If he could help by bringing her home, that's what he meant to do.

When he'd ordered the firewood and given instructions where to stack it, Grant leaned on his cane and admired the late-afternoon sunlight falling through the windows and lingering in her hair.

In different circumstances he guessed they might have been friends. Or maybe more? Beneath the defensiveness they seemed to bring out in each other, he sensed a powerful attraction. He hadn't been as drawn to a woman in years.

He looked at her with regret, then passed unnoticed behind the piano to the stairs leading down to his shop.

WHEN THE LAST NOTE died to silence, Teddi felt limp and comfortably empty.

"Bravo!"

Applause rippled through the lodge. Teddi stared at her audience with embarrassed surprise. She'd been so absorbed she hadn't noticed the gathering she'd created.

"Can you play 'Smoke Gets in Your Eyes'?"

Teddi laughed. "I think so."

"Anything we can sing along with," a squeaky tenor insisted. It was always the squeaky ones who wanted to sing along.

Long before the guests began drifting toward the dining room for dinner, Teddi had forgotten the disastrous lunch with Grant Sterling.

But she remembered later. Every hurtful word. Unable to sleep, she stared at a bar of moonlight creeping across her braided rug. And in the chilly night she saw Grant's accusing eyes and heard his sharp voice.

She closed her eyelids against the hot sting of unshed tears.

Everything he'd said was true.

Chapter Three

Teddi overslept, a situation she hated. Morning was the prime of her day, the time when she felt at her best. Worse, she awoke with a vague feeling of unease, as if she'd left something unfinished.

She yawned, swinging long legs over the side of the bed, then smiled, as delighted as she'd been as a child by the lacy ice crystals patterned across the lower windowpanes.

Slowly her smile faded as other images pushed at the edge of her thoughts: cold, white, deadly.

Jumping from the bed, she faced the wall and swung her arms above her head, beginning her stretching exercises. Forcibly clearing her mind, she concentrated solely on limbering hamstrings, quadriceps and the gluteus group. Smoothly, she moved into toe lifts, then ran in place, performing the simple yet effective series Ron Jensen, her coach, had designed for her so many years ago.

As much as she rejected the past, Teddi thought irritably, she was still controlled by it. Still doing specialized exercises she no longer required. Whoever had claimed habit ruled one's life knew what he was talking about.

After dressing quickly, she braided her hair into a loose coil that swung down the back of her sweater, then ran downstairs. The minute she saw her mother, she knew what she'd forgotten.

"I didn't order the firewood!"

Smiling, Marta ran her hands over the apron she wore like a uniform. "Don't worry. Grant took care of it."

"When?"

"He came by yesterday afternoon. While you were entertaining the guests."

"Oh." Moving behind the counter, Teddi processed a Visa card for a couple who were checking out while Marta registered a German family. She filed the paperwork, not looking at her mother. "Did Grant say anything about our lunch?"

"He said you were the prettiest thing he's seen and that you don't eat enough to keep a bird alive."

Teddi leaned her forehead against the cool surface of the filing cabinet. And when Marta added casually that she'd invited Grant to join them for dinner, Teddi winced.

"Mom? Are you by any chance matchmaking?"

Marta smoothed her white hair toward the bun on her neck, and her blue eyes rounded innocently. "Well, you and Grant would certainly make a handsome couple." She read the resistance in Teddi's expression. "Theodora, isn't it time you put Kip in the past and got on with your life?"

"I *am* getting on with my life." If that was true, then why hadn't she had a serious relationship since Kip? Wasn't that part of life? "I just haven't met anyone special," she added vaguely.

Concern flickered behind Marta's eyes. "No one special in six years?" she asked gently. "You're sure it has nothing to do with Kip?"

Teddi wished it was that simple. Her reticence to make another commitment involved Kip—her mother was right about that—but it was more than just Kip's death. She rejected the potential hurt of another serious relationship. The memories, the pain, the guilt.

Marta's accent thickened as it did when she was worried. "I don't think Kip would have expected or wanted you to mourn forever."

Was that what she was doing? Teddi lowered her eyes. No, her grieving had been intense, but it had ended years ago. She no longer mourned Kip. But she hadn't entirely let him go, either. Kip had become a protective shield between herself and the possibility of a new relationship with all its potential for hurt or disappointment. Until now, Teddi hadn't realized how manipulated she was by memory. Thinking about it gave her a headache.

She mumbled something about breakfast, then planted a hasty kiss on her mother's cheek and escaped the questions in her eyes.

After an aimless hour, she concluded there was little to do in a ski resort if one didn't ski. She knew this wasn't true, but at the moment it felt that way. Impulsively, she decided to go downstairs and have a look at Grant's shop.

But that presented a problem. She could take the elevator down one flight or take the stairs. Both choices offered difficulties. Since the accident, elevators had made her nervous, as did any closely confined space. The elevator was out. The stairs were better, but not much.

Teddi walked slowly toward Hans's "Celebrity Parade," which is how he referred to the staircase. Frame-to-frame photographs filled both walls. There were autographed pictures of Gerald Ford, Jack Nicklaus, Bill Cosby, Jill St. John and dozens of others. And numerous, endless photos of Teddi winning the Vail downhill, Teddi holding a large gold cup, Teddi flying through the gates. And Peter. And Kip. And probably, she guessed, Grant winning the NCAA championship, Grant at Lake Placid. She couldn't look.

At the foot of the stairs, she exhaled, then strolled along the carpeted hallway, examining the shops, some of which had been there when she was last home, many of which were new.

As she had no desire to actually enter Grant's ski shop, Teddi lingered outside the door, pretending an interest in an expensive outfit displayed in the window while she observed the interior.

Grant Sterling was making money hand over fist if the traffic inside was any indication. The ski-rental portion in back was doing a brisk business, with weekend skiers waiting in line to hand over their money. And two college girls were ringing up clothing sales as fast as they could pull the tags and write the tickets.

Teddi watched the smooth efficiency of the operation, then grinned suddenly, wondering which of the employees was Grant's executive administrator.

And she wondered if her mother realized she'd invited snow and fire to dinner, a combination guaranteed not to mix.

HANS AND TEDDI entered the dining room first, ordering drinks while they waited for Grant and Marta. They chatted briefly about the weather, the heavy influx of tourists, the need for more room maids before the Christmas holidays. Then Hans patted Teddi's hand and touched her shining hair.

"Are you happy, honey?"

"I think so," she answered. Realizing the reply was hardly definite, she amended it to a firm yes.

"No regrets?"

"I suppose everyone has regrets." Teddi responded after an uncomfortable silence.

Hans cleared his throat. "Have you ever thought about coming home for good?" The accent he had denied became more pronounced. "Your mother and I have been thinking about taking some time off. Maybe traveling a little and seeing how the world looks from the other side of the registration desk."

"Dad, I..." Teddi had dreaded this subject, had hoped it wouldn't arise so soon.

Hans raised a calloused brown palm. "I know you're doing well at the Alii, and we're proud of you. But your mother and I would like you to consider taking over the Edelweiss." He smiled and leaned forward to stroke her fingers. "Just think about it, okay?"

Teddi swallowed a sour taste. "I...I'll think about it. But Papa, please don't set your heart on this." A frown creased her forehead. She hadn't called her father "Papa" in years. "I have a good future with the Alii. I've made a lot of friends, bought a house..." Her voice trailed as she ran out of excuses. "I just...I don't fit in here anymore. I've built a new life..."

"I know." Hans made a soothing noise deep in his throat. "Just think about it. That's all we ask."

When she'd first learned Grant Sterling would join them, Teddi hadn't imagined she could possibly be glad to see him. But she was. Grateful for the interruption, she nodded toward the door with an expression of relief. "There they are."

She couldn't bear to look at the hope in her father's eyes. No more than she could bear the knowledge that she was disappointing him. Clenching her teeth, Teddi decided guilt was destined to be a constant companion during this trip.

Struggling with emotions she didn't want to appear on her face, she watched Grant pause in the doorway and lean to Marta's ear. They both laughed; then Grant grinned, bowed and gestured with his cane for Marta to precede him.

Teddi sighed. She'd hoped he wouldn't bring the cane. Or the phony limp. But he had. The mysteriously appearing and disappearing limp wasn't as pronounced as yesterday but was certainly more evident than the night of her parents' party. Irritated, Teddi narrowed her eyes and studied him as he wound through the dining room.

He had marvelous posture; she gave him that. He walked tall, carrying his shoulders back and squared, striding forward as if he owned the universe. Tonight he wore caramel-colored ski pants and a heavy sweater, the color as tawny as his eyes.

Chosen no doubt from the expensive line carried by Sterling ski shops. And, of course, he swung the cane, leaning on it when he paused to exchange a word with diners here and there. Teddi decided she was becoming fixated on his cane. She wasn't sure which annoyed her more, the cane itself or how dashing it made Grant seem. And it did; she admitted it. Of course, he knew that.

"Wouldn't a pipe serve just as well?" she murmured when he pulled out the chair next to her.

He gave her a long look. "I'm sorry, I didn't hear— What did you say?"

The force of his smile melted the sarcasm from Teddi's lips, and she experienced the discomfort of knowing she'd been one-upped. Or maybe he really hadn't heard her unpleasant remark. "Nothing," she muttered. For her parents' sake, she vowed to respect the truce his smile indicated.

It was harder to respect her own determination to remain indifferent to Grant Sterling. Beneath the table she felt his leg brush against hers. And she inhaled the fresh scent of snow and cold night air and the musky after-shave he wore. Why he affected her so violently on a physical level was a mystery, one that filled her with self-disgust.

A bevy of waiters clustered about the table, taking drink orders, fussing with the water glasses, offering menus.

Grant laughed. "What do you do to those poor waiters, Hans? Whip them between courses? If my employees worked like this, I'd own the world."

"You do, anyway." Hans grinned.

"Before I forget, there's a town council meeting on the fifteenth. Greene would like your ordinance committee to give a report."

Hans nodded. "Did Millard get in touch with you? There's a problem with the ski patrol, and..."

Teddi felt like an outsider. People and events had passed her by. Watching and listening as Grant and her parents discussed topics of mutual concern, she saw how interwoven their lives were. Grant knew more about the everyday fabric of her parents' lives than she did. Sternly, she reminded herself this was how she had chosen it. She didn't want to be involved with anything remotely connected with skiing. That part of her life was over.

When the waiter appeared to take their order, Marta smiled broadly. She reached for Hans's hand under the table. "No menus tonight," she said. "I made sauerbraten just for us."

"Marta!" Hans kissed her cheek as Marta beamed with pleasure. "We're in for a treat. No one makes sauerbraten like my Marta."

Her parents' easy affection was nothing extraordinary to Teddi; she took it for granted. Therefore, it was something of a surprise to notice Grant's expression.

He watched Hans and Marta with a half smile of quiet enjoyment, as if he were observing something rare and precious. The softness behind his eyes suggested a vulnerability that his craggy exterior hid well.

Teddi watched him curiously, then flushed and lowered her eyes when Grant caught her staring at him.

"A good marriage is like a rose that blooms forever," he said softly. "A rare treasure."

Teddi nodded slowly. Yes, she thought, he possessed areas of vulnerability. It shouldn't have surprised her. A man who required a prop to get through life would have soft spots in his personality. She glanced at the candlelit shadows lying in the hollows of his cheeks and idly wondered why the softness didn't show in his face. He had a strong face, the face of a man who feared nothing. It was curious.

"Tell me about Maui," Grant said, interrupting her thoughts.

Teddi recounted the Alii's growth and her modest contributions; she mentioned some of her more colorful friends and then spoke of the island's beauty and the water problems and a growing population and a cultural mix that was sometimes a blessing, sometimes a point of friction.

"It sounds like paradise," Grant commented when Teddi finished and Marta's sauerbraten had been happily consumed.

"It is. You should come see for yourself."

Grant's gaze locked to hers, and Teddi drew a quick breath. "Maybe I will." Then he glanced toward the crisp, cold night spreading beyond the windows and laughed. "On the other hand, this is paradise, too. How can you beat air that's crystal sharp and clean or the crunch of snow after a hard frost? It's tough to beat the exhilaration of a good run down the hill." A dark eyebrow arched, and he regarded her curiously. "Don't you miss it?"

"No!" But she remembered the icy patterns on her window and the breathtaking beauty of the sun sparkling on the mountain.

Hans and Marta exchanged a glance; then Hans leaned over his after-dinner brandy. "I have a favor to ask of you young people."

The rescue arrived not a moment too soon. Teddi sensed a dozen more questions in Grant's gaze. "Anything," she murmured.

"Dick and Greta Engles requested the night off, and I was wondering if you two—"

"Who are Dick and Greta Engles?"

Grant answered. "Dick drives the horses for the moonlight sleigh ride, and Greta directs the social activities."

"Oh." Teddi frowned. His tone of voice hinted that she should feel remiss for not knowing. Well, she wasn't buying any guilt trips from him. She looked at her father. "What would you like us to do?" she asked, though her sinking heart already knew.

"I have six guests signed up and no driver or director. Would you two mind filling in?"

Teddi flicked an accusing glance toward her mother, who smiled and blinked innocently.

Grant leaned backward in his chair. "I'd be glad to help out, Hans." Then he directed a challenging glance toward Teddi, amusement twinkling in his dark eyes.

Pride overwhelmed the unease nibbling at Teddi's nerves. "Of course I'll go," she agreed weakly. And she'd regret every cold minute.

After excusing herself to riffle through her bureau for long underwear and an extra sweater, Teddi collected the guests near the lodge door, while Grant drove to the stables to fetch the sleigh. And beneath her breath she asked herself how she'd gotten into this madness.

When the jingle of sleigh bells announced Grant's arrival, Teddi pressed her lips grimly and shepherded her charges outside. Frigid night air nipped her cheeks and bit at her nose as she directed the guests up into the hay-and-pine-bough-filled bed of the sleigh. Then she seated herself beside Grant.

He spread a heavy woolen lap robe over their knees and grinned. "Ho, ho, ho."

Teddi's eyebrows lifted, and her eyes narrowed. "Santa Claus, you're not." Santa wasn't this handsome, she silently admitted.

"Okay, Ansel. You can make this pleasant or lousy. What's it going to be?"

Startled by his directness, she looked into his cool eyes. It struck her suddenly that he was bending over backward to be pleasant. Since she'd done little to merit his effort, she assumed he did so for Hans and Marta. Could she do any less?

"We're going to have fun, Sterling," she replied. In a louder voice she called over her shoulder, "Isn't this a wonderful night?"

A chorus of agreement answered from the sleigh bed. The temperature hovered well below freezing, the air so sharp and icy it ached to breathe. She couldn't believe the tourists had actually paid money to be this miserable.

"Okay, it's a truce," Grant said softly.

She waved a mittened hand and elbowed him in the side. "Lead on, Santa; some of us are freezing." She pushed her hands beneath the lap robe and tucked her chin into the warm folds of her scarf.

Grant made a clicking sound with his tongue and flicked the reins over the horses' broad backs. The sleigh slid forward on waxed runners, the bells jingling merrily. A spicy scent of crushed pine filled the air.

Within minutes the symphony of sleigh bells and horses' hooves and the soft swish of the runners over the snow inspired someone to sing "Jingle Bells." The others spontaneously joined in a lusty rendition. "Frosty the Snowman" followed, then "Winter Wonderland."

"Christmas in November." Grant laughed. "Are you warm enough?"

"Are you kidding? I'm frozen." The cold penetrated her clothing and seeped into bones conditioned to Maui's hot beaches.

Grant slipped an arm around her waist and pulled her into the curve of his warmth. "Better?"

"Yes," she admitted reluctantly. Being pressed against the hard heat of his body did strange, exotic things to Teddi's nervous system. She was no longer certain if she was cold or hot. However, snuggling next to him stopped her from wishing she was somewhere else. Annoying as it was, she was acutely conscious of every small move he made. Breathing seemed more difficult, and her stomach had tensed into a bundle of fluttery impulses that she told herself she didn't understand.

The silvery mist of his breath settled on her lips as he leaned toward her. "Would you like to start over?"

She was cuddled firmly against him, side to side, thigh to hard thigh. There was no gracious way to refuse. A sigh released a white plume in front of her mouth. After a brief inner struggle, Teddi pasted a smile in place. "Hi. I'm Teddi Ansel. I understand you were a friend of my brother's."

Grant laughed and squeezed her glove beneath the lap robe. "I'll never forgive Peter for not introducing me to his sister."

"I can hardly believe that." Moonlight glinted off the silky curls beneath her cap as she shifted to look at him.

"Truce, remember?" Grant's gaze dropped to her lips, then rose to her eyes. "If we weren't agreed on a truce, I'd be tempted to point out what a prickly type you are. A tad bit quick-tempered." Amusement twinkled in his eyes. "But...since we've only just met, I'll simply say that Peter neglected to mention how beautiful you are."

Teddi ground her teeth. She listened to a few enthusiastic bars of "Over the River and Through the Woods," then blinked up at him with a sweet smile. "If I hadn't just met you, I'd be tempted to think you were much too interested in other people's business. But...since we just met, I'll simply ask how you and Peter knew each other."

"A point for you." A lopsided grin deepened the lines running from his nose to his wide mouth. "Peter and I were in the same fraternity at CU, and we were both on the ski team."

"I was on the ski team. How come you and I didn't meet?"

"As a matter of fact, we did. At a party for the team." He smiled. "I doubt you remember. There were over a hundred people on the ski team then—and you only had eyes for your fiancé, Kip."

Teddi pushed her chin deeper into her scarf. The conversation was skirting uncomfortably close to topics she wished to avoid. And she didn't see a tactful way out. After tugging her stocking cap down over her ears, she glanced up at his sharp, clean profile and shifted the focus to him. "Did you resent the regimen of training?"

"Hell, no. I loved it." Smiling, he guided the horses onto the snow-covered golf course. "From the time I was knee-high, I wanted to succeed at something, anything to prove I was worthy of taking up space. Since grade-schoolers don't think in terms of business, I thought about sports. I wasn't heavy enough for football or interested enough in basketball. Baseball was too much waiting and not enough doing. The day I discovered skiing, it was love at first sight."

Teddi nodded, remembering the first time she had glided on a pair of skis. It had been exhilarating. "How old were you?"

"About ten. I was living with the Andrews. In Denver." He saw the question in her eyes. "The Andrews were foster parents. I was lucky to be with them—they encouraged my interest in skiing and told me I could accomplish whatever goals I set."

"Well, you got what you wanted. You proved yourself," she said, thinking of the silver medal he'd won at Lake Placid.

"Have you, Teddi?" Grant asked, keeping his eyes on the horses' backs.

Immediately, Teddi bristled. "I think so," she said crisply, pulling away from the warmth of his thigh. "To my own satisfaction at least." She cast him a hard glance from beneath her lashes. "And that's the only opinion that really matters, isn't it?"

"Isn't that rather idealistic?" Moonlight washed the brown from his eyes and turned them to gold. "Like it or not, other people's opinions do matter."

The truce fell by the wayside. "What are you trying to say? That I've failed in some way?"

He reined the horses before the fire pit Hans had swept out earlier and laid with kindling and firewood. "You certainly didn't win, Teddi. You failed by refusing to compete."

She stared. A rush of anger bloomed scarlet in her cheeks. Her voice emerged in a hoarse whisper.

"Why do you keep pulling and pushing at me? What gives you that right?"

"You had a fabulous gift. And you wasted it; you threw it away." The lodge guests were jumping from the sleigh bed, stamping cold feet and rubbing their gloves over cherry-red cheeks. "Don't you ever look back and wonder if you could have won at Lake Placid? Ron Jensen said you were the best female downhill racer he'd ever coached. He thought you could win. The newspapers thought you could. How about you, Teddi? Do you ever think you might have won?"

"I don't want to—"

"Do you ever think about it, Teddi? And wish you hadn't thrown it all away?"

"Yes!" she hissed between clenched teeth. Hot tears glittered in her eyes; her mittens curled into knots. "All right, dammit. Yes, yes, yes!" A brackish taste rose in the back of her throat. "Sometimes I see the race in my dreams. I feel the mountain jolting up my legs, see myself flashing through the gates and flying over the finish line. And I wake up shaking and drenched with sweat. Wondering if I could have won! There, are you satisfied? Are you happy now?"

Flinging back the lap robe, she leaped to the ground, gasping as her boots sank into the snow. Then she reached for the basket of cookies and the thermoses of hot chocolate her mother had prepared as Grant set the brake and folded the lap robe.

Teddi's voice cracked in the cold air like a whip shot. "Do me a favor, will you?" Her eyes were as frozen as a winter lake. "If you're so damned set on making people face up to the truth, then leave that stupid cane in the sleigh!"

Spinning on her heel, Teddi kicked through the snow toward the huddled guests, then drew a long breath and summoned a false bright smile. "Having fun?"

They swore they were. They'd paid their money, and by God they'd convinced themselves this misery was fun. Smiling grimly, Teddi lit the fire to cries of gratitude, then poured steaming hot chocolate into Styrofoam cups.

From the corner of her eye she watched Grant Sterling. He sat on the high sleigh seat, staring after her. Good. She hoped he stayed there.

But of course he didn't. Shaking her head Teddi blew out her cheeks in a sigh of exasperation as she watched him climb from the sleigh and balance his cane in his glove. His face was tight and hard as he approached the guests sitting on the logs ringing the fire pit. Teddi noticed that although he carried himself tall and erect and didn't limp, he walked slowly, placing each step firmly before taking another. She rolled her eyes and bit her tongue.

Thankfully, he chose a seat as far from her as possible, though it meant facing him across the fire. When she discovered she was casting small covert glances toward him, Teddi jumped to her feet and led the group in campfire songs, hoping nothing in her expression revealed how upset she was.

Only Grant looked as if he was comfortable; he laughed and sang and chatted easily with the guests. Everyone else, including Teddi, was slowly turning blue. When she'd poured the last of the hot chocolate and passed out the few remaining cookies, Teddi sank to the log and tilted her head back, wishing she were a thousand miles from here. Overhead a canopy of stars winked from the night like brilliant chips of ice. A pale moon hung suspended above the black silhouettes enclosing the valley. It really was a magnificent night. The traitorous thought annoyed her.

Finally, Grant made a show of consulting his watch. "Well, ladies and gentlemen, I don't want the horses to catch cold..."

Laughing with relief, the guests rose and hurried toward the warm pine boughs filling the sleigh. Teddi expected Grant to kick snow over the fire, but he left that chore to her.

When she climbed up beside him, she discovered he'd placed the cane across the seat so it lay between them. That was fine with her. She jerked the lap robe over her knees and faced straight ahead, not looking at him.

It required a large quantity of willpower not to release a happy shout when the sleigh finally jingled to a halt before the Edelweiss's veranda.

The guests piled out, but before Teddi could dismount, Grant gripped her arm and forced her to meet his stare. "All right, Teddi. I'd hoped we could be friends for your parents' sake, but it isn't shaping up that way."

"Have you given it a chance?" She spit the words.

"Have you?" His fingers tightened on her arm. "What you need to understand is that I'm not going away. I don't give up. Every time you turn around, I'm going to be there. Trying to make you grow up."

Teddi gasped. "You're not my keeper! Just leave me alone."

"Not a chance. I care too much for Hans and Marta to let you push your head in the sand and hide. It's time somebody made you take a good, hard look at Teddi Ansel."

Teddi could not believe what she was hearing. She jerked away from him and stared in disbelief. "Who do you think you are? My life is none of your business!"

"I've been there, Teddi. You're letting the past beat you. I don't give a damn about that, except it's hurting Hans and Marta. That I *do* care about. And if I can do anything to stop it, I will."

"And your idea of helping my parents is to strike out at me?" She strangled on the words.

"Until you face the past, you can't face the future." Knots ran along his jawline. His eyes were cold and hard.

"I don't believe this!" Teddi struggled to climb out of the sleigh. The lap robe slid to the floor of the driver's seat, taking the cane with it. "Here," Teddi said sharply, throwing the cane up to him. "You don't want to lose this."

A dangerous glint narrowed his tawny eyes. "Striking out at me isn't going to change anything, Teddi."

A furious crimson pulsed in her cheeks. "Just forget about me, okay? Why don't you limp through one of the nearby pubs—maybe you'll find someone more to your liking. A lot of women fall for that pity routine."

Shivering so badly her teeth chattered, she spun and ran up the steps into the main lodge.

It wasn't until Teddi was wrapped in a thick flannel nightgown and curled into a tight ball beneath one of her mother's homemade quilts that she calmed down enough to realize she hadn't experienced any anxiety about the snow and cold.

She almost laughed aloud. In view of what she was feeling, anxiety would have been an improvement. Turning onto her side, she tried not to think of Grant Sterling, then gave it up as impossible. She couldn't think of anything else.

He was unforgivably rude and arrogant; he brought out the absolute worst in her. From all appearances, she did the same to him. Mentally reviewing their last exchange, she felt a surge of fresh anger. Here was a man who carried a cane he didn't need and who manufactured a limp when it suited him—and he was going to straighten out her life?

But behind her lids she saw his tawny eyes, his generous mouth. She felt the long muscular excitement of his thighs imprinted on her body.

"Dammit!" Teddi struck her pillow with a fist and flung herself on her back to stare at the dark ceiling. And for the first time in years, she deliberately tried to pull Kip up from her memory.

But the seeds of betrayal had taken root. She could no longer clearly visualize Kip's face or remember the sound of his voice. And if she admitted the truth, she hadn't been able to do so for years.

When Teddi finally slept and relaxed into dreaming, the man who drew her into his arms and covered her mouth with a sweetly passionate kiss was Grant Sterling.

Chapter Four

If Grant stopped by his ski shop on Monday or came upstairs into the main lodge, Teddi didn't encounter him. Not wanting to chance a meeting, she departed early in the morning and spent the day shopping and visiting friends. She didn't return until the sky turned leaden and hard pellets of snow swirled around her cap.

It was still snowing Tuesday morning. Teddi stood at the lodge window and stared at the white flakes blowing past the panes, determined to face down her uneasiness. A cold draft flowed over her hands. Combined with the wind-chill factor, the temperature had dropped to six below zero.

Closing her eyes, Teddi fervently wished she was sitting on the Alii's patio deck right now, sipping a piña colada and considering a dip in the pool. Turning from the window, she shook her head as a group of skiers departed the lodge, their skis balanced across their shoulders, their boots clumping loudly on the floor. They had to be crazy. All the bright dots zigzagging across the slopes had to be crazy.

"There you are, dear." This morning Marta wore wool slacks and a thick homemade sweater. She looked as warm as her smile. "Kelly called while you were having breakfast. I didn't have a chance to mention it before." Marta extracted a note from her bulging apron pockets. "She says she'll meet you at the Stube at eleven-thirty."

Teddi's face paled. The Stube was at Eagle's Nest, atop the gondola terminal on Vail Mountain. To reach the restaurant, one had to ride a gondola—a small, closely confined gondola—up the cable.

Smiling woodenly, she willed herself to walk, not run, to the phone.

Kelly's baby-sitter answered. "Mrs. Martin is out for the day. She's having lunch with a friend. Can I take a message?"

"No," Teddi whispered, "no message." She replaced the receiver, then leaned her forehead against the wall. She could phone the restaurant and cancel: "Please tell Mrs. Martin that her friend is terrified of the gondola and won't be joining her, thank you." Pride halted her finger on the dial.

She stiffened her shoulders and reminded herself that she'd known coming home wasn't going to be easy. And surely she hadn't expected to hide in the lodge without venturing outside, had she? Maybe she had. Well, that wasn't possible or practical. So where was her courage? What was she made of? Mush; she was made of mush. She didn't want to ride the damned gondola. But she did want to see Kelly. Reluctantly, Teddi zipped up her parka and tried to convince herself it couldn't be as bad as she was imagining.

Just getting there was a trial. The cold penetrated her clothing like hundreds of tiny icicles; the shuttle slipped and skidded on frozen roads.

Bending her head against the blowing snow, Teddi trudged toward the gondola terminal, then dashed inside, grateful for the warmth even as she continued to feel the sting of snow and frigid air against her cheeks. Slowing her steps, she stared at the shiny bright cars looping down the cable and rocking to a halt beside the passenger platform.

Her heart hit her toes. How could she possibly force herself inside one of those small cars? She wet her lips nervously and decided she couldn't.

When it was her turn, she stepped out of line and waved the man behind her into her place.

"First time you've seen a gondola?" The operator's college-boy grin admired the blond curls spilling beneath her cap; then he dropped his gaze to the black ski pants molding her hips like a second skin. "There's nothing to fear, fair maiden. We haven't lost a car in over a week."

Laughing at his joke, he watched the next gondola lurch through the opening; then he reached toward the doors as the car swung into position.

The noise of grinding gears and straining cable made conversation difficult. Turning, Teddi began to edge along the platform. Nuts to this. She'd call the Stube and cancel.

A hand grabbed her parka, then circled her waist, and Teddi felt herself being pushed into the gondola. She sat down hard and stared upward, her eyes brilliantly blue against a chalky face. The operator leaned in the door and winked. "Nothing to it. You'll see. Enjoy."

"Wait!" She snatched her hand back as the door closed, and she heard a clunk as the operator slapped the side of the car. The gondola rocked sickeningly, then lurched up the cable. "Oh, no," Teddi whispered hoarsely.

She sat knee to knee with a small boy. His mother sat beside him, and his sister occupied the seat next to Teddi. A roaring blasted in her ears, and then an eerie silence as the gondola whooshed free of the terminal and rose into a blinding white void of snow and sky.

Teddi clamped her fingers on the seat edge and drew a long, unsteady breath. She watched the children press their faces to the windows, heard them calling to their mother to see the valley dropping away beneath them.

If only they could have opened a window, she would have felt so much better. A light patina of perspiration broke over her body beneath her clothing. She lowered her face, uncertain what expression it held.

The children said something to her, and she mumbled a reply. She told herself there was enough air in the car. Intellectually, she knew this; emotionally, she reacted on a different level. She kept breathing deeply, assuring herself that she was safe. She could breathe; it wasn't like before.

Finally, mercifully, the gondola swished through the opening, and the snowy white blizzard dimmed to artificial light. The doors opened, and the children scrambled out, dragging skis and poles. Teddi put her head down and swallowed the warm terminal air in long gulps.

A man poked his head inside. "You getting out, gorgeous? Or going back down?"

"Out." Teddi gasped. Stumbling, she pulled herself from the car and staggered to the railing, leaning on it heavily. A burst of energy tingled through her fingertips, and a flush of triumph warmed her cheeks—until she remembered she'd have to ride the gondola back down the mountain.

THE THOUGHT BOTHERED HER all through lunch, distracting her from concentrating on what Kelly was saying. That, and the fact that they were sitting by a window. Every few minutes she caught herself staring at the wall of snow whirling beyond the glass. It had been snowing like this the day she and—

Kelly frowned. "Have you heard a word I've said?"

"I'm sorry." An urge to explain pressed at her lips, but pride wouldn't allow her to admit her phobia. She knew that's what it was. And she also knew she didn't want to discuss it. "Tell me about Jim's business."

"I did," Kelly answered patiently. "Teddi, are you all right? You look pale."

Skiers came and went, stamping snow from their boots, blowing on cold fingers, their cheeks a shiny apple-red. Teddi watched them and felt her throat closing.

"I have to go," she blurted out. The chair crashed behind her as she abruptly shoved back from the table. "Please forgive me, but...I have to go." Her eyes pleaded for understanding.

Kelly stared at her. "I wish you'd tell me what's bothering you. We used to talk about everything, remember?"

"I wish I could, but I can't." Teddi jammed her cap on her head and thrust her arms into her parka. "I'll call you." She bolted from the restaurant, her shaking fingers tripping over her zipper. Somehow she endured the nightmare descent in the gondola.

Her face was on fire when she reached the base
of the mountain. Her chest ached, and her throat
was raw from the effort to breath normally. Embarrassed, Teddi fled into the storm and flattened
herself against the side of the terminal.

Swallowing great gulps of frigid air, she closed
her eyes and raised her cheeks to the snow, which
stung her skin like tiny frozen needles.

It was all right now. She was behaving foolishly.
There had never been any danger. She could
breathe. After wiping her forehead with the back of
her mitten, she hurried forward, trying to look as
if she knew where she was going.

Beneath her boots the snow squeaked, as it did
when the temperature had frozen it brittle. All
around her rose the shouts of skiers comparing
runs, shifting equipment. Teddi shoved her hands
into her pockets and clenched her mittens into tight
balls, listening though she didn't want to.

"Did you ski Simba?"

"Nope. Too advanced for me. Did you try...?"

"I've had it, man. I'm freezing. Let's find a bar
with some hot spiced..."

"Someone said they're going to close the mountain; the weather is really getting rough and..."

"Maybe we can get in one more run before..."

Teddi had skied Simba; she knew it well. And she
could have told them where to find the best hot
spiced wine in town. And once she, too, would have

rushed to make one more run, no matter how bad the weather.

Oh, sweet heaven, she didn't want this. Where was the shuttle stop? She was sweating again, and feeling shaky inside.

"Look out, lady!" A pair of skis swerved by her boots. She had time to glimpse a blue cap and parka before they flashed past.

"Hey! Get outta the way." Levi's and a yellow jacket flew by her on the right.

Teddi blinked and stared around her. Many of the major runs ended at this point. They funneled through a wide gate and spilled the skiers out onto the nearly level snowpack where she was standing.

Dodging gliding forms, Teddi dashed to one side and pressed into the crowd of spectators. She drew a deep breath, fighting the inevitable; then her gaze turned up the slope toward the brightly clad skiers emerging from a curtain of snow. They flashed past her like the shimmering colors of a cool rainbow.

Unable to stop herself, she stared at them, mesmerized. Automatically, she judged their form and expertise. Most were amateurs, slowing with a determined snowplow. But here and there, an expert flew through the worsening storm, a symphony of grace and form.

One in particular caught Teddi's eye. This was no amateur, she thought, watching him with traitorous pleasure.

Edging slightly forward, she shaded her eyes from the driving snow and watched him gracefully flash into a sharp parallel turn, cutting back up the slope to slow his speed. The maneuver was executed so perfectly that Teddi felt an urge to applaud. Watching him was almost like watching a dancer, so effortless did he make it appear.

Apparently she wasn't the only person who admired the skier's skill and aplomb. Two college-aged girls standing behind her clapped their mittens together as the man slid to a halt a few feet away. He grinned at them, lowered his poles and leaned into a mock bow. Then he raised his goggles.

Teddi's eyes widened in surprise. Grant saw her, and his grin altered to a wary smile. "Teddi?"

She looked at him for a long moment; then her eyes slowly traveled down his body. She stared at the knee brace clearly outlined beneath his tight ski pants.

Teddi's shoulders slumped, and she exhaled slowly. She raised her eyes in an expression that asked forgiveness. "Damn," she whispered helplessly.

Chapter Five

Grant led her across the village to the parking garage and gave her a concerned glance as he opened the door of his Mercedes and watched her slide inside. She looked stunned, like a sleepwalker.

At first he didn't understand; then he did, and he studied her briefly before pushing the key into the ignition. She hadn't known about his knee. She must have thought he carried the cane for show or attention, or maybe she had imagined he was a flamboyant type with pretentions of grandeur.

The anger he'd been feeling since the night of the sleigh ride vanished. It was a relief to discover she wasn't the insensitive, hurtful person he had believed, an impression that didn't square with Hans and Marta's descriptions.

"Are you all right?"

"This hasn't been one of my better days," Teddi said.

She felt like a total and utter fool. The shock of discovering Grant actually needed the cane blotted all else from her mind. She scarcely remembered walking to his car, and she hadn't comprehended a word he'd said since.

Grant drove up a winding snowpacked road and parked the Mercedes before an architectural marvel of wood and glass carved into the mountainside. "I think you need a brandy and a warm fire."

Teddi nodded wordlessly. Inside, she peeled off her parka and cap, the movements wooden. Gently, Grant pushed her into the depths of a nubby white sofa; then he lit a fire in a soaring moss-rock fireplace and poured them each a snifter of brandy.

"I thought you knew," he said when he'd settled himself on the sofa beside her.

"No." Teddi drained the brandy in a single gulp and mutely extended the snifter for more.

"I assumed Hans and Marta had told you."

"If they did," she said wearily, "it was so long ago that I'd forgotten." She glanced at his leg, noticing he'd removed the brace at some point.

"Actually, I'm glad to hear it." A generous smile curved his lips, and amusement twinkled in his dark eyes. "Didn't you wonder why I carried a cane?"

Teddi winced. "I thought..." She drew a breath, not wanting to confess what she'd thought. "I thought the cane was just an affectation. I'm ashamed of the nasty things I said, Grant. I owe you an apology.''

Grant's smile widened to a grin. "Go ahead, Ansel. I can't wait to hear it. I especially liked the crack about women falling for the pity routine.''

She dropped her head and stared at the snifter. "I'm sorry.''

"What's that?'' Cupping a hand around his ear, Grant leaned toward her.

Teddi cleared her throat. "I said, I'm sorry.''

"Again, please. I'm loving this.''

She stared at him before a thin smile touched her lips. "I think you are.''

"I am.'' Looking at her, he assessed her expression, and then his grin softened. The firelight illuminating Teddi's strained face gleamed in his hair and along his jaw. "I'm relieved to learn you didn't know.''

"You must have thought I was the most insensitive—''

"Witch,'' he supplied with a laugh.

"—witch you'd ever encountered.''

"Close. There was a redhead I knew once, but that's another story.''

Teddi pressed her lips together, then gazed fully into his warm eyes. "Grant . . . thanks for being so understanding. I behaved unforgivably. You're being very generous.''

He brushed a wheat-colored strand of hair from her shoulder and watched it curl around his finger. "Actually, you've paid me a compliment."

The heat of his hand radiated gently against her cheek. "If I did, I don't remember. It seems all I've done is insult you." Drawing a breath, she glanced at him and then away. "I thought you were pretending to limp because you wanted some kind of neurotic sympathy."

"Which means you must have thought I didn't need the cane. Isn't that right?" Teddi nodded. "You'd understand what a compliment that is if you knew how hard I've worked not to limp. I'm happy as hell to learn you thought I was faking."

She looked at him doubtfully, uncertain how much of what he was saying was true and how much was an effort to ease her distress. The words blurted out before she could stop them. "What happened?" she asked softly.

Before answering, Grant refilled their brandy snifters, then leaned back against the sofa cushions. "A car accident, about a year after Lake Placid."

Carefully, Teddi examined his expression for a hint of bitterness. There was none. He spoke cheerfully, at ease with himself and the twists of fate.

"I'd persuaded a lady friend to stay overnight. The next morning was a day much like this one."

They both glanced at the blizzard whistling past the bank of two-story windows. "We should have known better than to drive, but she had to be in Denver that afternoon. We were hung over, in the middle of an argument, and trying to get down the mountain before the state patrol closed the tunnel."

Teddi nodded slowly, recalling an incident when she and Kip had behaved with a similar lack of good sense.

"We hit an ice bank," Grant continued. "The car bounced back on the road, slid across and bumped over the guardrail." A lopsided smile eased the next words. "I had a broken arm, two broken ribs, a concussion and a crushed knee."

"And your lady friend?" Teddi asked softly.

"It was one of those freak things. She walked away with a few bruises—and an overwhelming desire never to lay eyes on me again."

His laugh was infectious; Teddi returned his smile. "I'm sorry."

"It could have been worse—I could have broken both arms."

She stared and then laughed. "Were you always this casual about it?"

"Hell, no. When I finally recovered from the worst headache you ever imagined, I sank into a case of poor me's that lasted for weeks." His shoulders tensed briefly. "Skiing was the focus of my life. I had the medal and several lucrative commercials and promotional campaigns going. I was a pro, making money at it. Then suddenly it was all over. Before the wreck I was on top of the world, doing what I loved—I'd thought it would last forever."

A wince of pain shadowed Teddi's gaze. "I know," she said quietly.

"Then the doctors said I'd never walk again."

"Good God." She stared at his leg and then into his eyes. "How in the world did you get from 'never walk again' to here? Grant, we *danced* the other night."

"I danced—you resisted."

Teddi punched him lightly on the arm. "I thought you were some pretty-boy phony."

"Ansel, I'm crushed." Falling backward on the sofa, he clapped a hand over his heart. "I always thought a cane was dashing. I hoped it gave me sort of a David Niven élan."

Teddi grinned. "Well, it does. Sort of. Come on, Sterling; tell me who convinced you to throw away your wheelchair and walk."

Smiling, he rolled his head along the sofa back and looked at her. "I did. The worst words in the English language, the most defeating, are 'I can't.' One day I found myself thinking things like I can't ski again; I can't even walk into the kitchen and get myself a sandwich and a glass of milk. Suddenly I was thinking about all the things cripples can't do. And I didn't want any part of it.''

"It was that simple?"

He stared at her. "Good God, no. Come here, I want to show you something." Standing, he clasped her hand and led her into a wide hallway, down carpeted stairs to the lower level.

She released a low whistle of appreciation when he flipped on the lights. The basement was equipped with just about every Nautilus machine she'd ever seen. "This must have cost a fortune."

"And worth every penny. The day I decided to eliminate 'I can't' from my vocabulary, I bought all this and hired the best private therapist I could find."

"This room is better equipped than some gyms I've been in."

Teddi seated herself at one of the machines. From that angle she faced framed photographs hung at her eye level. After glancing around the room, she realized photographs were positioned in front of all the machines. They showed Grant playing golf and tennis, skiing, bicycling, fighting a kayak through foaming white water, swimming, rock climbing.

And then she saw his medal, framed against red plush. Sliding off the machine, Teddi circled the basement, discovering the medal could be seen from any machine, any angle. A spotlight glinted off the silver medallion, shooting a hard challenge to all areas of the room.

"This is . . ." Teddi spread her hands. "I don't know what to say." She stared at the photographs and the machines, thinking about what he'd put himself through.

Grant laughed. "You could tell me how impressed you are," he teased.

"I am." Admiration softened her eyes. "Did the doctors really say you would never walk again?" Looking at him standing before her, she could hardly believe it.

"When they said that, Teddi, my knee was shattered. I couldn't support any weight at all on that leg." He shrugged. "What they didn't figure on was humanity's will to conquer adversity."

"I think you're being modest. This has much less to do with humanity than with Grant Sterling."

They stared at each other for a long moment. Afterward, Teddi couldn't remember who stepped forward first. She only knew she was suddenly in his arms, pressing her forehead against his shoulder as his strength enfolded her. Closing her eyes, Teddi wound her arms around his neck.

"You must feel so proud of what you've accomplished," she said, leaning back to look up at him. Her body tingled and caught fire where their hips pressed together.

"I'm not there yet," he said, looking at her mouth. "I still carry that damned cane when I've overexerted or when I don't know what sort of terrain to expect."

They gazed into each other's eyes for what seemed an eternity. Teddi felt as if she were drowning in warm liquid caramel. Her fingers tightened on his shoulders as his eyes slowly traced the curve of her parted lips. And she felt his muscles swell beneath her fingertips as his arms tightened around her.

Then she closed her eyes as his mouth brushed hers in a gentle, almost-questioning kiss.

But when she opened her eyes and looked into his, she read the same mounting desire that rocketed through her own body. And she felt breathless as his thumb brushed her mouth and she realized she wanted him to kiss her again.

This time his mouth was firm and hard. And when Teddi parted her lips, his tongue seized the invitation to explore. He claimed her mouth with a bruising urgency, and when he released her, she leaned aginst him, shaken.

"I've wanted to kiss you from the moment we met," Grant murmured against her forehead.

Smiling, Teddi pressed her cheek against the rough weave of his sweater. "You probably won't believe this, but I've wanted you to."

Clasping his hands behind her waist, Grant leaned back and smiled down at her. "Will you stay for dinner?"

There had never been a question. Teddi cocked her head, her blue eyes sparkling. "Who does the cooking?"

"I do, Ansel. I make it a rule never to trust a woman with a steak."

"Oh? Well, I happen to believe men should be barred from making salads. They gunk on too much dressing."

"I like lots of dressing. Then it's settled?"

"Lead on, Sterling. Where's the kitchen in this place?"

Grinning, he looped a silky strand of hair behind her ear. "I'm amazed. I always believed women had a sixth sense about kitchens. I thought you could home in on them in a minute."

"That is outrageously chauvinistic. It's like saying all men have a sixth sense for bedrooms and hot tubs."

"The bedroom is upstairs, and the hot tub is by the fireplace."

"If your female clientele knew about this, you'd be drummed out of Vail."

"As long as they keep coming to Sterling ski shops and bringing their husbands' credit cards."

Laughing, they mounted the stairs, and Grant ushered her into a large homey kitchen. "Recognize anything?"

"So this is what a kitchen looks like," Teddi placed her hands on her hips and looked around with wide eyes.

Grant flipped on the Jenn-Aire, then guided her toward the fridge, his large hand warm on her back. "Allow me to introduce you to a refrigerator and—voilà!—the lettuce crisper."

Chatting easily, they prepared steaks, a salad and microwaved baked potatoes. Teddi carried plates and silver to a dining table positioned before floor-to-ceiling windows. Outdoor spotlights shone into the snow, making little headway against the early darkness. She studied the storm, thinking it had worsened if that was possible.

"I'm not sure I can get you home in this," Grant remarked.

"I think it's gotten worse." A blinding wall of snow blew past the panes. "Exactly where are we? I'm afraid I wasn't paying much attention when we drove up here."

"We're above Lionshead."

Which was a long drive from the Edelweiss, Teddi realized. In order to reach the village, they would have to travel down roads sabotaged by numerous hairpin curves.

"Picture Nichol Run in your mind." Grant didn't have to ask if she'd skied Nichol; of course she had. It was an advanced run named for five wicked turns that only an expert dared attempt. "Nichol swings to within sixty feet of my balcony."

Now she knew where they were. And she knew trying to reach the Edelweiss in this storm was about as appealing as another gondola ride. Grant's thoughtful gaze suggested he was thinking the same thing.

"This is going to sound like a proposition, but would you mind if I spent the night?" Her cheeks brightened to the same rosy pink as her sweater. "Driving in this storm scares me to death." She drew a breath. "You have a guest room, don't you?"

"I was going to suggest the same thing." For a long moment his tawny eyes lingered on her lips, then rose to meet her gaze. "Yes, I have a guest room. If that's where you want to be."

"I . . ." Teddi wet her lips as her heart accelerated. "I think I should call home."

Her mother's voice was weak with relief. "We were getting worried."

It was silly, but Teddi felt uncomfortable about telling Marta she was spending the night with Grant. She needn't have worried; Marta made the suggestion for her.

"Stay where you are, dear. The roads are sheer ice. Wait until morning—by then the snowplows and the sand trucks will be out."

Grant took the phone from her hand. "Marta?" He cradled the receiver on his shoulder while he poured coffee and snifters of Amaretto. "I'll take good care of her. In fact, I think the safest plan would be to wait until spring, when all the snow's melted off. I'll bring her back in, oh, say, April or May." He listened for a moment, then laughed. "Okay, we'll see you sometime tomorrow. Tell Hans not to shovel the veranda. I'll do it when we get there."

"That was nice. Offering to shovel the veranda," Teddi said when they were settled before the fire. "Is there anything you can't do?"

"Not much. Especially if I remember to wear the brace." He crossed his ankles on the coffee table and stretched his arm along the back of the sofa, gesturing her nearer.

Without hesitating, Teddi curled close to him. After a moment she looked up. "Are you supposed to wear the brace all the time?"

Grant smiled against her hair. "You sound like Marta."

"Well?"

"No, I only wear it when I'm doing something that might place an undue strain on my knee. Like skiing or a lot of walking."

They sipped their coffee and Amaretto; then Teddi asked the question she'd wanted to ask all evening. "Grant? Can you still ski cross-country?"

His body tensed, and she sensed the depth of his disappointment. "Yes," he insisted stubbornly, "I can." Then his shoulders relaxed. "But it wears me out," he admitted softly. "I'm limping for days afterward."

"I'm sorry." She thought of the career he'd had in cross-country, of the medals he'd won.

"So am I," he answered simply.

Teddi twisted in his arms to look up at him. "You didn't seem to have any trouble skiing downhill."

"Downhill isn't as tedious," he said. The warm scent of Amaretto flowed between them. And the intensity in his dark eyes told her he wasn't concentrating on their conversation.

Teddi lifted her eyes to his thick lashes, and her breath caught. She took the snifter from his fingers and placed it on the coffee table; then she curved her arms around his neck and rested her forehead against his. "Grant Sterling, you're very special; do you know that?"

"Why? Because I cook a terrific steak and can stand upright?"

Teddi's fingers wound into his hair, and she nipped his lower lip. "No," she murmured, fitting herself against his body. "You stand out in my mind because you're the only man I ever met too dumb to know what an executive administrator is."

Chuckling, he trailed kisses along her jawline and then her throat. His large hands opened across the back of her sweater, pressing her against his chest. "Don't tell me about dumb, Ansel," he said in a husky voice. "It was you who drowned a perfect steak in A-1 Sauce."

"I saw you glop more Roquefort into the bowl," Teddi whispered, darting her tongue along the curve of his lips.

They smiled at each other, and as their smiles faded, Teddi knew the teasing had ended. When he kissed her again, her breath quickened, and her heart raced against his. She framed his cheeks with her fingers and moaned softly when the heels of his palms pressed against the swell of her breasts. When she drew back from his mouth, her breath was as ragged as his.

Grant's hands stroked her hair back from her face. "My sixth sense tells me this is the moment I should show you the hot tub." His voice flowed over her like rich, dark honey.

"I think your sixth sense is right." Her own voice emerged low and throaty.

Grant nuzzled her ear. "I'll race you."

Teddi laughed softly, feeling a tingle spread over her body. "No fair. You know where it is."

The hot tub occupied a large room behind the living room, sharing the same fireplace. Two of the walls were glass, affording an unobstructed view of the valley. On a clear night the village would have twinkled like a chain of Christmas lights. Tonight the lights blurred behind a blowing curtain of snow.

"This must be a magnificent view."

"It is," Grant assured her with a wicked grin.

Teddi looked over her shoulder and discovered him admiring the curve of her ski pants molding her buttocks. "I meant out there."

"I've seen that view... I'd rather look at you." His gaze moved slowly over her body; then he pulled her into his arms, covering her mouth with a long lingering kiss.

Eyes locked to his, her heart beating with a mounting urgency, Teddi slowly raised her sweater over her head, then stepped out of her ski pants. Her fingers shook slightly with a nervousness that came from not having been with a man for six long years. Suddenly she wondered if she would be inhibited, if she could perform as a complete woman. She cast a quick panicked look at Grant, then felt herself relax. Looking at him, she realized she couldn't turn back; she wanted him. And it felt so right, so absolutely right.

Standing before him in lacy bra and panties, she summoned a smile. "Your turn."

Grant's reddish-brown curls vanished under his sweater, and Teddi stared at his well-developed athlete's chest.

Beneath a light sprinkling of dark hair, his muscles were hard and sharply defined. She closed her eyes briefly and swayed, feeling a rush of desire.

Swinging his legs over the side of the tub, Grant slipped into the water, then stretched his arms along the rim and smiled expectantly. When Teddi stepped out of her undergarments and stood before him with a mixture of shyness and pride flickering in her eyes, he stared at her, then whispered hoarsely, "My God, you're beautiful."

Teddi glowed with pleasure as she stepped into the heat and bubbling steam and lowered herself into the water. She ran her hands up his body from his hips to his shoulders and stretched out, letting her body sink down to cover his. Her nipples hardened into small pink buds as her breasts crushed against his chest, and his mouth claimed hers with a sudden urgency that matched her own. A soft moan came from her throat as she felt his strength against her stomach, hard and demanding. His hand cupped her head, guiding her lips against his in a kiss that shot arrows of fire through her nerves.

There was nothing gentle or teasing in their kissing now; they sought each other with a passion as intense as the storm raging beyond the glass. And beneath the heated water, their hands rushed to touch and explore, to give as well as receive the greatest pleasure. Grant groaned against her lips as her hands stroked his chest, then moved lower, and she gasped when his fingers gently rolled her nipples into an aching need.

Denied for so long, Teddi's body responded quickly and passionately to his skilled touch. An urgency that was nearly painful tensed her muscles and tore at her breath. Her fingers gripped his slippery shoulders, and her hair trailed in the water as her head fell backward beneath the rain of kisses showering her throat. His fingers slid from her breast to her waist and set her skin on fire. And when his hand cupped her center, she cried out, every nerve begging for release.

She called his name, but he waited until they were both gasping, until their kisses were frenzied with need, until touch and taste shifted and mingled and became one. Then, his large hands circled her waist, and he guided her onto him.

Teddi's fingers tightened on his shoulders. And her eyes closed as a small cry broke past her parted lips. "Yes. Oh, yes, Grant, yes."

They moved slowly together, exploring each other's needs before establishing a rhythm unique to themselves. Their hunger for each other was too compelling to sustain patience for long. Finally, his arms tightened convulsively around her, and his head dropped to her breast. She held him tightly and cried his name as the world exploded behind her eyelids.

Later, they wrapped themselves in fluffy over-sized towels and stretched out on the living-room carpet in front of the fire.

Grant sighed contentedly and reached to fill their glasses with chilled white wine. Propping his head in his hand, he leaned on an elbow and smiled down at her. "The pity routine got you, didn't it?"

Teddi knocked his elbow out from under him. "Not a chance." She grinned.

He laughed, his dark eyes skimming the towel wound around her hair, then dropping to the cleft showing above the towel wrapping her breasts.

Teddi smiled up at him. "I love your body," she said softly. She loved the long, graceful lines, his tight, smooth skin across chest and thighs. She loved the sharp definition of muscle and sinew and his craggy outdoor face. And the way the firelight gleamed through his hair and heightened the gold in his eyes.

Rising on an elbow, she offered her mouth for a lingering kiss, then relaxed, feeling at ease for the first time since she'd set foot in Colorado. She decided she could fall asleep in about two blissful minutes.

"Teddi?"

"Hmm?" The blizzard howled around the corners of the house, but it didn't frighten her. Not now. She felt safe and warm and protected. Nothing could hurt her here.

His hand stroked along her back, warm and possessive. "Isn't it time we talked about it?"

"About what?" she asked drowsily.

"The avalanche."

A violent cramp knotted her stomach, and her eyes flew open. She bolted upright and stared at him.

"No! I—" She bit off the words and examined his calm, expectant expression. Grant Sterling was not a man who would understand "I can't." He was watching her. And waiting.

Suddenly she felt trapped.

Chapter Six

"Teddi?"

In the silence Teddi heard the blowing snow whistling around the corners of the house, listened to the fire popping cheerily in the grate. And she heard the panicked rush of her pulse thudding in her ears. She cast Grant a quick glance, a mute plea in her eyes. But no reprieve was forthcoming. Grant squeezed her fingers encouragingly and waited, patience softening the lines that bracketed his mouth.

"Take your time," he murmured, stroking her hand.

Time, she thought resentfully. Time was supposed to heal, but it hadn't, not entirely. Time had eased the pain, yes, but returning to Colorado—and Grant's questions—had freshened old wounds by freeing the painful memories she'd boxed in a safe dark corner of her mind.

Drawing up her knees, Teddi circled them with her arms and stared into the fire. She wished to heaven that Grant Sterling was a different kind of man, a man who would accept "I don't want to talk about it." A brief flash of anger darkened her eyes. She suspected it was no accident that he had chosen this moment to question her, when she couldn't escape and when, after making love with him, she didn't want to.

"It was a beautiful morning," she said finally. Her voice emerged in a harsh whisper. Each word felt as though it was being ripped from her heart. "We knew a storm was coming, but we thought we'd be home before the worst hit the valley."

Closing her eyes, Teddi surrendered to an onslaught of details she had believed long forgotten. A light crust had topped the snow pack that morning, and where the sun had touched the snowy meadows, a million crystals glittered like diamonds. The day had smelled of spruce and pine, and the air was cold and sharp and invigorating. In her mind she could still hear the whispery swish of their skis gliding over the crust.

Tightening her grip on her knees, Teddi wet her lips and stared blindly into the fire. "We were cross-country skiing. Peter and Kip had promised to wait for me if I fell behind."

Their shouts and laughter echoed from the far reaches of her mind. Kip and Peter had worn the scarlet caps they'd purchased for the Olympics, and sleek black pants with red racing stripes. Each time she'd looked up to shout a reply or exchange a joke, her heart had expanded with love and pride. She had watched them showing off for her, cutting skillfully through the pine-edged meadows and speeding beneath snowy overhangs, and she had wanted both of them to take the gold even though it was impossible. They couldn't both win. That's what she'd been thinking when the first flakes of snow pelted her cheeks.

"When the snow thickened," she continued softly, "we decided to go back. We were just beyond Pine Overhang...and then..." A thick band tightened around her chest, and her stomach knotted. "Then we—we heard a noise like a faraway rumble."

If she lived to be a thousand, Teddi would never, ever, forget that sound. It was impossible to describe, unlike anything she'd heard before, like a small resonating rush that snowballed swiftly into a deafening roar that stabbed the ears and heart and soul with a dread that would reverberate through a lifetime of nightmares.

"We stopped. I was about a hundred yards in front of Kip and Peter."

For moments, they had stood frozen like statues captured in mid-motion, staring up at the mountain, at trees toppling before the speeding weight of a huge wall of snow. Then they had burst into frantic motion, bending over their skis, pushing hard on the poles. And Teddi had known, had known with an icy spill of terror, that they wouldn't make it. Sound roared all around her, trees snapped with sharp popping cracks. She had stopped and turned to look behind her, wanting to say something in the seconds remaining to them, wanting to say all the things she knew she would never have a chance to say again.

Her voice sank to a scarcely audible whisper and hoarsened with emotion. "Peter or Kip, I don't know who, called my name, and then..."

Tears blurred the logs in the fire. She didn't see Grant reach to stroke her shoulder to feel her body trembling beneath his fingertips. Her eyes widened, and she stared into memory, seeing the surge of snow rushing down on her. And she remembered the horror of watching oblivion smashing toward her, knowing there was no escape.

"Then I was in it. Buried in a wave of snow." Teddi squeezed her eyes shut, but the scenes continued to unreel behind her lids. She lost both skis immediately. And her poles. She'd glimpsed a flash of scarlet off to one side, and then white, only white. Closing around her, burying her, smothering sight and thought. "I'd read somewhere that if you were caught in an avalanche, you were supposed to swim. So I swam. I tried to swim with the flow of it, tried to stay near the top."

But within seconds she'd lost all perspective. She hadn't known if she was swimming upward as she was supposed to or if she was digging down into the body of the slide. It had surprised her that she continued to hear the roaring; she remembered telling herself she must be near the surface if she could hear the roar. She remembered clinging to that hope.

"And then it just—it just stopped." She stared at nothing, seeing white. Cold, smothering white. A dark, dirty white, the color of fear. "My hands were in front of my face. I could move them enough to make a small hole."

By pushing and digging frantically, she had enlarged the hole and watched it ice over as her breath spilled into the space. And then silence had descended, a silence as mind-shattering and replete with dread as the roar had been. She'd held her breath and listened to the terrible silence until the wild beating of her heart reminded her that she was still alive.

"I tried to dig out," Teddi said when she could again force herself to speak.

But she hadn't known if she faced up or down, if the snow had tumbled her as it had tumbled the pines and stones. Her lower body was trapped by cold, silent weight, and she couldn't move anything but her hands and one shoulder.

"I didn't know which way was up. And I thought my leg was broken. All I could do was keep breaking the ice in the breathing hole and try to make it larger."

In those first seconds after the snow stopped moving, she had lain very still, weak with the simple joy of still being alive. Then, as the seconds stretched into minutes, hope had been replaced by mounting panic.

She remembered thinking the snowstorm would fill in their tracks. They would vanish without a trace. Soon, very soon, she would gulp all the air in the small hole and she would suffocate. An icy cold froze her face, seeped through her clothing, and she recalled stories of lost skiers who hadn't been found until the spring melt-off. She didn't have enough air. Most of all, she remembered gasping and panting and knowing she didn't have enough air.

"Oh, dear God." Teddi gripped her knees and rocked back and forth. Tears streamed down her cheeks, but she was unaware of them. In her mind she was beneath Pine Overhang again, buried in the snow, her body encased in a deep chill of ice and fear. Utterly helpless. "I couldn't breathe. I...could not breathe.

"I think I blacked out, or was starting to." She couldn't remember. "Then something hit me in the back. Later I learned it was a ski pole. Two skiers had seen the whole thing."

They had found her by jabbing their poles into the snow. After digging frantically, they freed her head and administered mouth-to-mouth resuscitation. One of the skiers had a walkie-talkie, and he summoned help. The sequence of time and events had never unraveled correctly in Teddi's memory. It had seemed an eternity before the helicopters descended through the falling snow, but Hans told her later they had appeared on the scene less than fifteen minutes after receiving the call.

"Funny," Teddi whispered. "I thought my leg was broken, but it was my arm." She rubbed a hand across her eyes. "I was there when the rescue team found Peter and Kip."

She had been too numb with shock to cry when the rescue team had found them, but now she reached out to Grant, who held her against him. She had never been able to release her emotions—until now.

Without speaking, Grant tenderly stroked her damp hair away from her face. Then he said, "Finish the story, Teddi."

"That's all." Her throat ached, and her lungs burned as if she'd only now been rescued.

"No," he said gently. "I think there's more."

She stared into the patient depths of his eyes and hated him. "You won't quit, will you?"

"No." The back of his hand followed the firelit line of her jaw.

"What more do you want?" Anger steadied her voice, a hot, unreasonable anger that swelled her breast and trembled through her body. Her blue eyes flashed. "Do you want to know what it feels like to be alive by a trick choice of fate? I couldn't look in the mirror for weeks, knowing I'd been saved and they hadn't. I wondered if the minutes spent saving me had cost Kip and Peter their lives. That's what guilt is like. That's the rest of the story."

She pushed to her feet and shouted at him, "I lived, they died, and I don't know why. Do you understand that?" She stared at him furiously, hating him for dredging up her pain. Suddenly the anger fled as swiftly as it had come, and she covered her face with her hands. "I'm sorry." She drew a long shuddering breath. "I'm not angry at you, Grant. I'm angry at the world, and confused... I don't know why it happened, or why I lived and Peter and Kip didn't."

Gently, he guided her to the sofa and spread a colorful afghan over her lap. "Go on."

"Go on?" Astonishment flared in her eyes. Then a tired smile brushed her lips. "You're incredible, do you know that?"

He pulled her into the curve of his arm and rested his chin on her hair, looking into the fire. "I know it all has to come out."

Maybe he was right. Relaxing into his arms, Teddi glanced at the snow melting down the windowpanes. The ordeal of remembering the avalanche had left her mentally exhausted, but it was an honest fatigue, not the nervous, anxiety-ridden weariness she had dreaded. She felt cleansed somehow.

"There isn't much more to tell," she admitted. "A few days after—after the funerals, I tried to ski. But I couldn't. Everything reminded me of that day. There was no point in competing; nothing seemed to matter anymore. So I withdrew from the Olympic team."

She waited for Grant to comment. When he didn't, she continued. "I transferred my credits from the University of Colorado to the University of California at San Diego. I didn't want to ever be cold again."

"Which explains why you took the job in Maui rather than coming home?"

Teddi nodded. "It doesn't snow in Maui," she said quietly.

"Okay, you hate cold and snow. You're afraid to ski. Is there anything else from the past that's still threatening?"

A frown pleated Teddi's brow. She wasn't sure she liked his phrasing. Haltingly, she admitted her fear of closely confined spaces.

Grant shifted on the sofa and cupped her chin, turning her face upward. "Now the question becomes, What are you going to do about it? Are you going to allow the past to beat you?"

"We're back to that old story?" Teddi asked.

"That's what this is all about, isn't it?" Grant's thumb traced the full curve of her lips, and his eyes softened.

Teddi looked at the craggy strength in Grant Sterling's face, and she thought of the exercise machines in his basement. And suddenly she wanted to be a person he could admire. "I came home," she said simply. "It's a big first step."

"Yes, it is." His lips grazed the delicate curve of her eyebrow as his hands slid to her waist. "It's a beginning."

"Grant?" Teddi inhaled the sweetness of his breath and felt her pulse accelerate as the heat of his hands spread over her body. "Make love to me," she whispered against his lips. "I need you to make love to me."

A low groan issued from his lips; then he lifted her in his arms, and Teddi buried her face in his neck as he carried her up the staircase and into a loft bedroom. Snowy light filtered from the skylight and spread a wintry shimmer over a quilted bedspread.

Gently, Grant placed her on the quilt. "Don't go away." In a moment he had a fire crackling in the bedroom fireplace. Then his weight depressed the bed as he knelt and slowly opened Teddi's towel. The firelight warmed her skin to a combination of rose and ivory. "You are so beautiful," he murmured huskily.

"Hold me." Teddi opened her arms and bit back a cry of pleasure as he came into her arms and stretched out beside her. She needed his strength now, the solid feel of sinew and muscle and power. As if sensing her needs, Grant wrapped her in his warmth, stroking her trembling body with long teasing slides of heat. And although Teddi felt the same tense building of urgency that she'd experienced earlier, he refused to be hurried.

"Shh," he whispered against her throat. "Slowly, Teddi, slowly."

"Grant . . . please . . ."

"Not yet. I want to love all of you." Kisses trailed up the back of her knee, kindled fires along the inside of her thighs. His mouth teased along her stomach, discovered the soft valley between her breasts.

And when Teddi thought her quivering body would explode with passion, when her breath was ragged and labored, when her body strained against him and their kisses had become wild and frantic with desire, then he came to her.

She called his name and clung to him and gave fully of herself as she'd never done before. Today had been one of the most intensely emotional days she could remember. And much of it she had shared with this man, this wonderful man who teased her body into molten fire. As Teddi moved closer to the release only he could give her, she stared into his tawny golden eyes and knew she was where she wanted to be with the man she wanted as she had no one before him.

Later, Teddi nestled in Grant's arms, waiting for her breath to return to normal. She thought about the day. It should have been a disaster, but she didn't view it that way. Right now, she felt totally relaxed, fulfilled in a manner that surprised her.

Being in Grant Sterling's bed, cradled by his strong arms, seemed utterly right. She gazed drowsily at the snow curved over the skylight. Instead of appearing threatening, the cap of snow impressed her as protective, cozy almost. It was crazy. Had anyone told her a week ago that she would be glad, happy even, to be trapped in a blizzard, she would have laughed and thought him mad.

Smiling, she snuggled closer to Grant, then closed her eyes and slept more soundly than she had in years.

WHEN GRANT FELT the even rise and fall of Teddi's back against his chest, he eased away and quietly slipped from the bed.

Downstairs, he poured a glass of milk and gazed at the stormy night through the kitchen window. It had been a long time since he'd brought a woman home, longer since he'd felt an emotional stirring. He didn't relish one-night stands, but Vail was a tourist town, a holiday village where brief encounters were the norm rather than the exception. For a man who wanted permanence and continuity, it was easier not to get involved.

"Maui," he said softly, shaking his head. He couldn't visualize Teddi Ansel in Maui. In his mind's eye, he continued to remember her flashing down the mountain, taking the gates like a pro. This was where she belonged, in Vail.

And if he were honest with himself, which he usually was, he wanted her in Vail as much for his own sake as for Hans and Marta's. He suspected this was a woman he could become very fond of, very fast. There was a strength in Teddi Ansel that he admired, and a sharp bright intelligence coupled with humor.

There were also flaws.

Snapping on the basement lights, Grant entered the gym and seated himself at the rowing machine. As he usually did when he couldn't sleep, he applied himself to exercise, hoping the machine would

ease the ache from his leg. The day had been stren-
uous. And the memory of being confined to a
wheelchair wasn't all that distant. Talking about the
car crash had reminded him of the frustration of
being helpless.

Bending to the mechanical oars, he thought
about the months he'd wasted trying to understand that which was not within understanding. The
months of resenting stairs and high countertops and
the pitying glances of friends and strangers. The
blank spot in his mind where his future had been.

Whatever strength had propelled him to overcome his handicap and carve a new life lay within
Teddi; he sensed it as strongly as he sensed the lingering fragrance of her perfume on his body.

Pausing, he wiped his forehead, finished the milk
and leaned over the oars, pushing his feet out before him.

Hans and Marta had told him about the avalanche years ago. He'd guessed the experience was
the reason Teddi had refused to compete at Lake
Placid. What he hadn't grasped was the extent of
the past's hold on her. He hadn't realized she was
still fighting ghosts. The idea of the past ruling the
present was so alien to him, he made the mistake of
imagining it was so for everyone.

And yet wasn't he guilty of the same thing? Here
he sat, rowing like a madman in the middle of the
night because he still thought of himself as a crip-

ple in some corner of his mind. Because the specter of the wheelchair was never far away.

The thought startled him, and he grimaced. Perhaps no one was ever really free of the past. Perhaps he would always fear helplessness, always search for the stability and permanence he had lacked as a child.

Stepping from the machine, Grant carefully placed his weight on his leg, smiling when it supported him.

The key lay in acceptance, he decided. And in understanding oneself, the limitations and the possibilities. At least that's how it had worked for him. And it could work for Teddi Ansel, too.

When he returned to the bed, he eased her into the curve of his body and gently brushed a long strand of gold from her cheek. He'd always been a sucker for small wounded creatures.

A grin curved his lips as he imagined her anger if she'd known he'd thought of her that way even for an instant. Then his hand cupped her breast, and he thought how snugly she fit into his body.

Yes, he decided, he could become very fond of her, very rapidly.

Chapter Seven

Teddi awoke to the delicious scent of freshly brewed coffee. Overhead the snow had slipped from the skylight and opened a path for the bright morning sunshine to spill across the quilt. Smiling, she swung her feet to the rug, got into Grant's bathrobe and stepped to the balcony railing. "Is that coffee I'm smelling or nectar of the gods?" she called.

He grinned up at her, his russet hair still damp from the shower. "Coffee. And breakfast is almost ready. Get a move on, Ansel, I don't cook for fun."

She yawned and stretched. "Wonderful. Make mine sunny side up. With lots of tomato juice."

"It's scrambled and orange juice. Cook's choice."

"I think the cook's choice is burning." Teddi laughed. When Grant had vanished beneath the balcony overhang, she showered, dressed in her pink sweater and dark ski pants, then descended the stairs.

Grant was buttering toast. "About time," he observed with a mock frown. "If this is going to be a regular thing, we'll have to buy a louder alarm clock. You didn't even wriggle when the buzzer went off."

Teddi took the butter knife from his hand and finished the toast. "Is it going to be a regular thing?" she asked lightly, not looking at him.

"Ansel, I'm offended. What are you, the love-'em-and-leave-'em type? If I'd known you wouldn't respect me in the morning, I'd have played harder to get."

Teddi laughed. "Is this another pity routine?"

"Certainly. I wine you and dine you, loan you my favorite towels, offer you a bottle of my second-best brandy, listen to your life story, submit my body to your wild and wanton ways, and what do I get for it?" He rolled his eyes toward heaven and spread out his hands. "She turns coy on me. Can you believe it? I do everything I can to impress this woman, and she turns coy. What does it take, Lord?"

"A little begging would be nice," Teddi teased. She sat down and surveyed the table. There was enough food to feed half of Vail. "What's this business about your second-best brandy? Who gets your first-best brandy?"

He filled their glasses with chilled orange juice. "I'm saving my first-best brandy for a special occasion."

"And what constitutes a special occasion?"

"I'll know when I see it. Now, eat your eggs. And yes, this is going to be a regular thing. I don't believe in one-night stands. I'm not that kind of guy." Innocent brown eyes caught the morning sun and flickered gold. "You aren't the type of woman to take advantage of a man, then abandon him, are you?"

Teddi choked on a bite of toast. "Are you suggesting that I took advantage of you?"

"Didn't you hear me begging for mercy?"

She laughed merrily, feeling so happy she couldn't believe it. She'd always thought of herself as basically a happy person, but she had never felt like this, as if everything were right with the world and there was nothing so serious that it couldn't be handled.

"So. What do you think?"

"About what?"

Grant put down his knife and fork and tilted his head toward the ceiling. "Give me patience. She's a pretty thing but a little thick in the head." After releasing an extravagant sigh, he lifted his eyebrows and looked at Teddi's wide smile. "About us, Ansel. About us."

"What about us?"

"Are you trying to drive me crazy before I've even finished my juice? Us. You and me. That us. It's nice having someone to make coffee for in the morning. It's nice waking up with you snoring on my shoulder."

"I don't snore!"

"Yes, you do. What I'm trying to say is that I like having you here. Do you like being here?"

Sunlight tinted his hair a deep rusty color and heightened the gold flecks in his gaze. Tiny lines crinkled around the smile in his eyes. But it wasn't his handsome face that caught at Teddi's breath. It was the vulnerability behind his eyes and at the edge of his voice. Suddenly she knew that Grant Sterling hadn't opened himself to many women.

"I like being here," she answered softly.

"Well, thank God, a quasi-commitment." He placed a hand on his heart. "I knew a woman who hates cards and jazz couldn't be all bad."

Teddi's tone sobered. "Grant, I can't just move in here; you know that, don't you?" She saw the disappointment behind his smile and felt it in her own heart. Leaning forward, she touched his hand. "In a week I'll be returning to Maui. I'm not sure my parents would understand if I moved in with you." She met his eyes. "Although I'd like to. But this trip was for them."

"I know. To tell you the truth, I'd forgotten about them." He squeezed her hand. "Of course you have to stay with them. For now."

"Grant...this is happening so fast. Two days ago I didn't even think I liked you, and now..."

"I don't believe that, Teddi." He wasn't touching her, but she felt him with all her senses. He looked at her, and a warmth spread upward from her stomach. "From the moment we met, something began to happen. Can you deny that?"

"No," she whispered. She stared into his eyes and felt a flush of color pink her cheeks. And heaven help her, she wanted to make love to him again. She wanted those powerful arms holding her; she wanted his lips on hers, and ...

"If you don't stop looking at me like that," Grant said in a husky baritone, "I'm going to forget I promised Marta I'd shovel the veranda. Your eyes remind me of columbines in spring."

His reminded Teddi of a tiger's eyes, a smoldering mix of caramel and gold. She considered telling him, but it would have sounded impossibly corny. A laugh bubbled past her lips that she could even think in such terms.

An expression blending amusement and impatience darkened Grant's eyes. "Ansel, why are you laughing? I'm trying to be romantic here. How many times has a man compared your eyes to columbines? I could have said something trite like cornflowers or sapphires. But no, I try to be precise, and what do you do?'' He grinned at her. "You're supposed to pay attention and be impressed. You're not supposed to laugh.''

She couldn't help it. "Columbines? In the spring?''

"The state flower. You know. Blue and white and delicate?'' He tossed his napkin at her.

"I'm impressed. Honest.'' But she was laughing so hard tears welled in her eyes. It wasn't just what he said; it was a silliness born of sheer happiness. Everything made her smile.

"Okay,'' he sighed. "So much for romance in the morning. Come on, woman. I cooked; you get to clean up. While you're being domestic, I'll shovel out the driveway.''

After filling the dishwasher and putting away the place mats, Teddi collected her coat and cap and met him outside the garage. "Here, I brought your cane. After this exercise, you're going to need it.''

He looked deeply into her eyes, then kissed her nose. "Thanks.''

When they arrived at the inn, Marta examined their smiling faces, and a slow knowing look stole across her expression. Her face pleated in a wide smile. "Have you two eaten breakfast?''

"An hour ago. Did Hans leave the shovel in the shed?''

Marta nodded, then Grant left. When he was gone, Teddi hugged her mother. "No questions, okay?"

"It's different between you two. A mother knows these things."

"He's very special, isn't he?"

"Yes, he's very special. And so are you."

Teddi followed her mother inside. "Mom...do I snore?" Marta smiled and lifted an eyebrow as Teddi's cheeks bloomed with twin flames. "Well, do I?"

"Why do you think we gave you the bedroom farthest down the hall?"

IT WASN'T until the guests began to drift toward their rooms to change for dinner that Teddi realized she hadn't eaten lunch. The registration counter had gotten busy about eleven o'clock; then there had been a contretemps with the cleaning staff, followed by a minor emergency in the kitchen.

"What time is it?" Teddi asked, pressing her hands against the small of her back and stretching.

Marta pushed aside her ledger and removed a pocket watch from her apron. "Six-thirty."

"I could eat a horse."

"Oh, that reminds me." After rummaging in her apron pocket, Marta triumphantly produced a note. "Grant left this for you. He wants you to have dinner with him."

"You read it?" Some things never changed. Smiling, Teddi shook her head, then opened the note. In it, Grant invited her to dinner at Le Petit Chat, a French restaurant new to Teddi. He'd also invited Hans and Marta. "Aren't you going to change, Mom? We only have an hour."

"We'd like to go, dear, but I'm afraid I'm behind on posting the books, and Hans has a new mystery from the book club..." Marta's voice trailed into an elaborate shrug. "Maybe next time."

Teddi grinned. "Are matchmakers always this transparent?" Her mother's innocent look didn't fool her for an instant. After bending to place a quick kiss on her mother's cheek, Teddi ran upstairs to shower and change.

After considerable thought, she chose a blue velvet suit and a cream-colored silk halter top. Columbine blue, she thought with a smile as she smoothed the skirt over her hips. Leaning to the mirror, she applied a light-pink lipstick, then tucked a strand of hair into the shining cluster of curls pinned atop her head. After glancing at her watch, she sprayed her wrists and throat with Chanel No. 5 and stepped back from the mirror.

She looked lovely. The side slit in her skirt emphasized the long, slender line of her legs, and the silk top curved softly over her breasts. For once her hair had behaved perfectly. But it wasn't her physical beauty that pleased Teddi as much as the glow that radiated from within. Tonight her skin appeared luminescent, her eyes a sparkling blue. She looked vibrantly alive, like a woman hugging a delicious secret. Laughing at her foolishness, she dropped a white fox coat over her arm and closed the door to her room.

Grant was waiting at the registration counter, teasing Marta about her bulging apron pockets. Tonight he wore an Italian-cut dark suit, a white silk shirt and a maroon Gucci tie. As Teddi crossed the lodge, he shifted weight, and she noticed the outline of his knee brace beneath his pants leg. Her heart expanded. And she smiled as she noticed the women who drifted toward the dining room, giving Grant a hard second look.

He turned as Teddi approached and released a long, low whistle as an appreciative stare swept from her legs to the golden curls crowning her head. "Exquisite," he murmured gruffly. "Did you have those legs yesterday, or are they new?"

Teddi laughed, and her eyes danced. "An ivory-and-gold cane? Very David Nivenish." He looked so dashing and urbane, he might have stepped from a movie set.

"Too bad it isn't a sword cane. I have a feeling I'm going to have to fight off every man in Vail once they get a look at you."

They smiled deeply into each other's eyes, and Teddi felt a flush of heat spread over her breast. She tried—and failed—to recall the last time a man had affected her like this, on so many different levels. Not only did she respond to Grant physically, but intellectually, as well. She liked his light humor, admired his courage and appreciated his generous nature.

A tiny frown marred her brow as she slid into the Mercedes and wrapped her fox coat around her. Was she ready for an emotional attachment? And how sensible was it? They could have no future. In a few days she would be returning to Maui, while Grant's life would continue here. Yes, she had talked about the avalanche, and yes, the thick layer of snow blanketing the ground didn't seem as threatening as it had when she'd first arrived.

But essentially nothing had changed. She'd been vastly relieved to learn from Marta that dining at Le Petit Chat would not require a gondola ride or elevators. She was evading her father's request that she consider taking over the inn. And there was still Kip and the lingering guilty conviction that by having a serious relationship with someone else, she was betraying his memory and somehow making his death meaningless. Her intellect told her it was ridiculous to deny herself happiness, but on a deeper emotional level that was how she felt.

It was all so confusing. In a way she would be glad to return to the Alii, where such thoughts seldom troubled her, at least not on a conscious level, where she had to deal with them.

"Tired?" She asked Grant when they were seated at a candlelit table, facing each other across snowy linen and gleaming silver. The restaurant resembled a French country château outside, and was subdued elegance within. A tuxedo-clad waiter placed their drinks before them, then withdrew to stand vigil near floor-to-ceiling windows overlooking the valley. Tonight was clear and cold; a new moon drifted from behind a single cloud.

"A little," Grant admitted.

"What else did you do today besides shovel mountains of snow?"

"I arranged my schedule to be free the next few days. I want to spend every minute with you. We have a lot of work to do."

"Work? This is my vacation, remember?"

He didn't smile as she'd expected he would. "Teddi...I've thought a lot about the conversation we had at the Ore House." Seeing the smile fade from her lips, Grant leaned forward and covered her hand. "I understand your reasoning better now than I did—but the bottom line is the same." His eyes held hers. "You're running away," he said gently.

"I thought you understood," she answered quietly, withdrawing her hand.

"I do. I understand that you endured a terrifying ordeal, one that's left scars. I also know that Vail is where you belong, not several thousand miles away."

"You're wrong," she said, forcing her voice to remain light. "I have a good life in Maui. Lahaina is my home now."

His thoughtful gaze made her uncomfortable. "Is it your home from choice? Or has the past pushed you there?"

"Does it really matter? I'm happy, Grant, I like my life as it is."

"Yes, it matters. If you genuinely prefer Maui to Vail, Teddi, then okay. I'm sorry for Hans and Marta, who need you, but...okay." Teddi winced but said nothing. "But if you've convinced yourself that Maui is where you want to be because you can't face what happened here, that isn't okay."

Irritation flared in her eyes. "Look, it's my life. Can we just leave it at that?"

"No. Because it isn't just your life. Your parents are affected, too." He looked as if he wanted to say something more but changed his mind. "All I'm asking is that you look into your heart and examine your motivations. Do you want to beat the past or be controlled by it?"

She stared at him. "The past isn't controlling my life," she snapped.

"Isn't it?"

She continued to stare into his steady gaze while a flood of detail crowded her thoughts. Elevators, the gondola ride, the dread of cold and snow, her parents' desire that she take over the Edelweiss. The stubborn resistance that had stiffened her spine evaporated, and her shoulders dropped.

Grant saw the change. "Teddi," he said, "can you honestly know whether or not you're in Maui by choice until you've beaten the memories that initially sent you there?"

It made sense. She hated it, but what he said was true. "Are you always this relentless, Sterling?"

"Always." A smile curved his wide mouth. "So, are you ready to go to work?"

"You and me—crusaders against the past?" she asked with a wobbly smile.

"Something like that, yes."

Once again, Teddi thought about the machines in his basement. Her blue eyes flicked at the cane propped against the windowpane. She hadn't bargained for this when she had decided to fly home. She hadn't anticipated Grant Sterling.

Lifting her eyes, she stared into his direct gaze and knew something important hung in the balance. Their relationship would go in one direction if she agreed to his challenge, would quietly fade in another direction if she ran away.

"I want to beat it," she said impulsively. She wanted Grant to approve of her, to admire her as she had admired him when she stepped into his private gym. And maybe, just maybe, she wanted to admire herself again. The thought raised a startled expression to her eyes. Until this moment she hadn't realized her self-esteem wasn't all it could be.

Grant's face lit with delight. Both hands reached across the table and squeezed hers until she laughed in protest. "I knew you would," he said enthusiastically. "Ron Jensen said you had the spunk and courage of a winner."

"Ron said that?"

"He believed it. And so do I."

The waiter cleared the dessert plates and served them glowing snifters of brandy. "All right, where do we begin? I assume you have a plan?" Teddi asked.

Grant grinned. "I have for you the Sterling Four-Day-Wonder Plan."

Teddi groaned around a smile. "I was afraid of that."

"Tomorrow we'll ski the beginner's slope."

Her heart contracted. When she could speak, she gazed at him with a shaky half smile. "I'm not ready for that, Grant. I'm sorry, but...can't we sneak up on it?"

He looked at her for a long moment. "Then we move to Plan B. A reintroduction to winter sports. Tomorrow we'll ice-skate. Is that agreeable?"

Teddi probed the idea in her mind, seeking any hint of discomfort. "Agreed," she said finally. Curiosity lightened her voice. "Can you skate?"

"I don't know, I haven't been ice-skating in years."

Not since the car accident, Teddi interpreted. Well, if he was willing to attempt skating with his weak knee, so would she. Her eyes narrowed, and she regarded him with a challenging tilt of her head. "I used to be pretty good," she teased. "This may be a humiliating experience for you. Are you sure you want to subject yourself to being shown up on the ice?"

He laughed. "Spoken like a true competitor, Ansel. But you should know that I am the personification of grace itself, a symphony on ice. I will skate rings around you. Unless..."

"Unless?"

"Are you going to wear one of those skimpy little outfits?"

Teddi grinned. "Scoop neck with a skirt that barely clears my fanny."

"I'm done for," Grant groaned. "I won't be able to think, let alone skate."

"Are you sure you still want to do this?"

His eyes dropped to her moist mouth, then lingered at the hint of breasts peeking above her silk halter. "I wouldn't miss it for the world."

They were still laughing and teasing each other when Grant parked the Mercedes in front of the Edelweiss. He guided her into the darkness away from the veranda door and kissed her, his warm lips an electric thrill melting the frigid night air.

When he released her, he turned her fur collar up to frame her cheeks and stared down into her eyes. "I wish you were coming home with me tonight," he said hoarsely.

"So do I," Teddi whispered. She felt herself being pulled into the warm caramel depths of his gaze. When his thumb brushed her mouth, a tidal wave of desire rushed over her, leaving her weak-kneed and breathing shallowly.

Grant wrapped her in his arms and laid his cheek against her hair. "I like you, Teddi Ansel. I like you a lot."

She inhaled the warmth of his skin and the sensual fragrance of his after-shave. "I want you to like me," she said into his collar.

"I do." Drawing back, he kissed her lightly on the nose. "Now, run inside before you catch cold. And, Teddi . . ."

She turned at the doorway and smiled back at him. He stood in the spill of light falling from the open door, leaning on his cane and looking "too good to be true" handsome. "Yes?"

"I hope you can't sleep. I hope you toss and turn all night, missing me." A wide grin opened beneath his twinkling eyes.

Teddi laughed. "Being a kinder person than you, I hope you sleep like a baby."

His grin widened. "I probably will. Some crazy woman's snoring kept me awake all last night, so I'm tired."

She threw a snowball at him, then pushed her hands into the sleeves of her fox coat and watched until the car's lights vanished around the curve.

She managed to maintain her high spirits through a nightcap shared with her parents, but when she was in bed and allowed herself to contemplate the Sterling Four-Day-Wonder Plan, her heart sank.

At some point, Grant would expect her to strap on skis and face the mountain. Did she really want to do that? Just thinking about it tightened her body with tension. Grimly, Teddi forced herself to relax. She'd take it one small step at a time and see how it went.

Chapter Eight

The Dobson Ice Arena was warm inside; dozens of skaters glided about the smooth ice, keeping time to the lilting organ music that poured from overhead loudspeakers.

Teddi spread her arms, then tightened into a spin as the music built to a crescendo. She was enjoying herself. The cool air rising from the ice brought color to her cheeks but wasn't uncomfortably cold; the music was light and upbeat, and after a wobbly beginning, she was handling herself well. Thanks to the exercises designed by her ski coach years ago, her ankles were strong and her body supple.

Gliding out of the spin, she bent over her skates and made another circuit of the rink, searching for Grant. When she found him, her lips curved in a mischievous grin, and her eyes twinkled. She spun neatly to a halt, spraying tiny ice chips over his skates.

"Still clinging to the rail, Sterling?" She spread her hands on her hips and made a clicking noise with her tongue. "Is this the same man who promised to skate rings around the competition?"

Grant's tanned face pulled into a sheepish frown above a white cable-knit sweater. "I just remembered what's wrong with this plan—I hate ice-skating."

Teddi's grin widened. "Well, I'm having a grand time. Watch this." Showing off, she swung into a figure eight. "What do you think?"

"I think you're rubbing it in," he said sourly.

Teddi laughed. "I think you're right. Come on; let's sit down and have some hot chocolate." The relief on his face made her chuckle.

"Thank God," he breathed, lowering himself into a chair. "Who suggested this?"

"You did," Teddi reminded him. "If you hate ice-skating, why are we here?"

Grant placed a hand on his chest and managed an expression of noble self-sacrifice. "I did it for you, of course. Some men climb the highest mountain, some swim the deepest sea—I strap blades on my feet and go ice-skating."

In a way, he was telling the truth. Being here provided Teddi with a much-needed reminder that winter sports didn't have to be dreaded. Skating was a long way from skiing, but it evoked a subtle attitude adjustment. She blew on her hot chocolate and smiled at him over the rim of the cup.

"Why haven't you ever married?" she asked suddenly. Immediately she regretted the impulsive tactlessness inherent in the question. On the other hand, Grant was handsome, successful and charming—and she was curious.

"Is this a proposal?"

"No, just curiosity." Pink blossomed in her cheeks. "And don't tell me you haven't found the right girl; that's so trite."

"As a matter of fact, I did find the right girl. Twice."

"Twice?"

"I've met two women whom I thought I could be happy with."

"What happened?"

He shrugged. "I met Susan in college, in my jock days. She didn't want to marry a jock, so that was the end of it. Deirdre didn't believe in marriage; she wanted to live together but without the ultimate commitment. I believe in marriage and commitments, so that was the end of that."

Teddi regarded him thoughtfully. "You're an unusual man, Grant Sterling," she said softly.

"When I marry, Teddi, it'll be forever. I want a tough lady who can weather the tough times and be there at the finish." He looked at her. "Trite or not, there aren't many women today who want to commit to the old traditional values. Now, how about you? You're beautiful, bright as hell and sometimes adorable.'' He grinned at her lifted eyebrow. ''Why haven't you married?''

''I don't know,'' she said slowly. ''I haven't had a serious relationship since—since Kip. I haven't allowed anyone to get close enough to discuss marriage.''

Grant examined her curiously. ''Are you still mourning Kip?''

''No, it isn't that.'' Teddi bit her lip. Then the words emerged in a rush. ''I just feel guilty. Like I have no right to be happy if he can't be.'' She spread her hands in a helpless gesture. ''I can't explain it. I just—maybe I'm afraid to love again. Maybe that's part of it. Afraid to suffer the pain of loss again.'' She couldn't believe she was saying this, laying herself raw before him.

''You want forever, too,'' Grant observed softly.

''That's part of it. But there aren't any guarantees!''

Grant reached to take her hand. ''Teddi, people have to make their own guarantees. That's what a commitment is. But before you can make a valid commitment—'' he paused and looked deeply into her eyes ''—you have to forgive yourself for surviving the avalanche.''

She stared at him with wide eyes. With his usual directness, he'd plunged to the heart of the matter and given it a voice. And it sounded so patently ridiculous when stated aloud. "I suppose so," she responded vaguely before changing the subject. "There's a square dance at the lodge tonight. Will you come?"

Grant studied her until Teddi squirmed uncomfortably in her seat. "No," he said finally. "I'd like to, but I have to attend a town-council meeting tonight. Will you meet me later for a drink?"

A subtle shift had occurred in the mood between them; Teddi sensed it immediately. She also sensed she wouldn't be comfortable joining the after-ski groups for drinks. "Not tonight," she said lightly. Then, because she didn't want him to think she was avoiding Vail's nightlife, she added, "Maybe tomorrow night." Pushing away from the table, she smoothed down her short red skirt and glanced toward the ice. "There's time for one more circuit, I think. Coming?"

Grand shook his head and smiled. "I'll stay here. Where I can admire you in safety."

At first Teddi was very aware of him watching her. Then she succumbed to the music and the smooth ice beneath her skates and gave in to the joy of long, graceful strides. Moving easily, her golden hair flowing behind her, she tested her body in a series of maneuvers that gradually became more demanding. At the finish, she spun to a stop before Grant, her cheeks flushed and her eyes glowing with the pleasure of knowing her body had met the demands she'd placed upon it.

A hunger stole across Grant's countenance, and Teddi read the desire in his stare. "You are so beautiful," he said softly. "So incredibly beautiful."

A thrill of electricity shot through Teddi's body, and suddenly she wanted him with a need that was almost tangible. She whispered his name and saw the understanding in his eyes as he read the urgency in her stare.

"You guys gonna sit here all day? Or do you want more chocolate?"

Teddi blinked at the waiter; then she exchanged a long look with Grant, and they both laughed. She removed her skates while Grant paid their check; then she looped her hand through his arm, and they dashed for the shuttle.

At the shuttle door, Grant said, "Sure you won't change your mind about that drink?"

She was tempted. But the square dance would last until midnight, and they had a full day planned for tomorrow. "I think I'll pass," she murmured against his lips.

Grant drew back slightly to look deeply into her eyes. "Tomorrow night?"

Teddi knew what he was asking, and a wave of weakness swept her body. "Tomorrow night," she whispered.

Teddi planted a hasty kiss on Grant's chin and jumped aboard the shuttle. She leaned back in her seat, staring at the condos and restaurants without seeing them. Things were moving fast, very fast, between her and Grant Sterling. *Slow down and think,* Teddi cautioned silently.

Neither she nor Grant was the type to indulge a quick vacation fling. So what was the status of their relationship? With a sinking feeling, she suspected Grant saw it as long-term. But was that possible? A long-term relationship would involve a tremendous upheaval for one of them. The sudden panicky tension that caught her breath told Teddi she wasn't ready for that.

But if their relationship was short-term, then what was the purpose? She turned that dismaying thought around in her mind, reaching the reluctant conclusion that there really was no point in seeing him again.

But she knew she would; she couldn't help herself. Even recognizing the futility of any long-term commitment, she knew she couldn't stay away from him.

Teddi sighed heavily. All right, her emotions were becoming entangled; she admitted it. When the time came, it wasn't going to be easy to say goodbye to Grant Sterling.

She leaned her head against the cold windowpane. What should have been a simple vacation had become confusingly complicated. She felt swept up in emotions and events she wasn't sure she welcomed.

Her thoughts skipped ahead to the Royal Alii and the life she'd built for herself there. Immediately, a calmness smoothed the crease from her brow. There was nothing threatening about life in Lahaina.

An impish voice reminded her there was also nothing particularly exciting or challenging. And no man there to send her pulses racing or to ease the loneliness of the long, warm nights. She sighed again and wished life could be simple.

GRANT USUALLY ENJOYED town-council meetings. Being part of Vail's inner community and having a choice in its future satisfied a need to be part of something greater than himself. But tonight his mind had drifted.

When he and Hans stepped outside into the sharp night air, Hans stretched, then gestured toward the Spotted Pony, a small bar and grill the locals frequented as it was too rustic to attract many tourists. "Have time for a beer?"

"Sounds good." The routine seldom varied. After each council meeting, Hans asked if Grant had time for a beer as if they hadn't stopped at the Spotted Pony once a month for the last four years. Smiling, Grant opened the door to a blast of warm air and the thumping sounds of a country-western trio singing of lost love and bad times from the back of the room.

They took their usual chairs against the wall and waited for Fred Ames to deliver tall foaming glasses of the Swiss ale he ordered especially for Hans.

"Well?" Hans asked, pushing back his cap. "What do you think of Bill Myers's proposal to spot zone the Upper Valley?" He looked at Grant shrewdly. "Or did you even hear a word of Bill's speech?"

"I'm against spot zoning. God knows I've said so often enough."

Hans nodded, then asked too casually, "How's business? Are all the stores doing well?"

"The Denver shop is a little off this season, but the other two are thriving." Grant smiled fondly as he recognized Hans's concern. "I'm not worried about business, Hans. Sales couldn't be better. I wasn't thinking about my business tonight; I was thinking about yours."

"The Edelweiss?"

"Have you talked to Teddi about taking it over?"

Hans looked into his ale. "She's happy in Maui. Maybe there are too many memories here." After a pause he added, "She agreed to think about it."

"You should tell her, Hans; she deserves to know." In the bright lights shining from above the bar, Hans looked his age. Tanned wrinkles fanned from his eyes, and tufts of white hair curled from the edges of his cap. Grant thought he looked tired.

"No, Marta and I agreed it would be wrong to pressure Theodora. If she comes home, it must be because that's what she wants, not because she feels an obligation to us."

Grant didn't agree, but they'd had this discussion before, and he knew the strength of the Ansels' feelings. Frustration and that old feeling of helplessness darkened his eyes. "How is Marta? Is she taking her medicine?"

"Yes." Hans removed his cap and pushed his fingers through his hair. "But I worry about her. She does too much, works too hard."

"What does the doctor say? Is there any danger of another heart attack?"

"There's always the danger, but..." Hans spread his hands. "Doc Carlson thinks it's time we retired. But you know Marta—there's no slowing her down."

Grant knew neither of them wanted to see the Edelweiss end up in the hands of strangers. He leaned forward. "Hans, I urge you to reconsider. Tell Teddi about Marta's heart. She'd take the Edelweiss in a minute if she knew."

"I know. But she'd take it for the wrong reasons." He drained his ale. "We want her to be happy."

"Dammit, Hans, this is Teddi's home. If she'd face the past, she'd be back here in two minutes flat. You've seen how she looks at the mountain. With fear, yes, but with yearning, too."

"Marta said the same thing." Hans shrugged and met Grant's eyes. "We don't know how to help her," he admitted softly. He touched Grant's hand, then got to his feet. "She's a good girl, Grant. Maybe someday..."

After Hans said good-bye, Grant ordered another beer and watched the country-western trio without really seeing them. He'd promised not to mention Marta's condition, and he respected Hans and Marta too much to break his word to them. But keeping silence strained his capacities.

For him, the phrase "I can't" had broken through the paralyzing grip the car accident had exerted. He felt certain that knowledge of Marta's heart attack would do the same for Teddi and begin the healing process she had delayed so long. But he had to honor his friend's request, so that option was not open. He would have to find something else.

Frowning, he tasted his beer and absently tapped his fingers in time to the music. He thought of Marta and pondered the Sterling Four-Day-Wonder Plan. He hoped to hell it worked. And he hoped he could continue to keep a light tone with Teddi and not betray Hans and Marta's secret.

PART TWO of the Sterling Four-Day-Wonder Plan involved snowmobiling. Teddi tugged her cap down over her ears and smiled at Kelly and Jim, who were examining the snowmobile they had chosen. Buck and Judy, friends of Grant's, were already seated in their snowmobile, studying the map marking the route Grant had selected.

Grant cupped his hands around his mouth and shouted for their attention. "We'll stay together, agreed? No side trips alone." He checked his watch. "We should reach Buck's ranch about noon. Did everybody bring their swimsuits? Good." He climbed into the snowmobile in front of Teddi and smiled over his shoulder. "Okay—wagons ho!"

AT FIRST, Teddi wasn't certain whether or not she liked it. An uneasiness pricked her nerves as they left the village behind and roared down a mountain valley. Then, gradually, she was seduced by the crisp, sparkling day and the heavy scent of snow-clad pines. Tiny screams and giggles came from the snowmobiles behind them, and the men shouted back and forth. Beneath the soft rumble of the engines, she could hear the snowmobile runners slicing through the snowpack.

Without realizing exactly when the transition occurred, she moved from apprehension to enjoyment. When Jim and Kelly shot past them, hurling snowballs in their direction, Teddi jabbed a finger in Grant's back.

"Are you going to let them beat us, Sterling? Step on it."

He grinned at her as Buck and Judy edged nearer, shouting good-natured insults. Then all three snowmobiles spread out side by side, zooming across a snowy meadow dotted with moguls. Grant aimed the snowmobile for one of the hills.

Teddi's smile froze on her face. Her eyes widened as the hill rushed toward them, and her fists clenched. "No," she whispered soundlessly.

The snowmobile crashed through the top of the hill; snow shot up and momentarily blinded her. Teddi felt the freezing crystals showering her face, and her heart jumped erratically. She couldn't breathe. Oh, Lord, she couldn't breathe!

The snowmobile crested the small hill and careened down the other side. Before Teddi's strangled scream died in her throat, the machine had leveled out, and the pale wintry sun was melting the crystals on her cheeks. She went limp against Grant's back and closed her eyes, sucking in great gulps of cold air.

Then they were smacking through the top of the next mogul, and she was freshly blinded by flying snow. The roar of the snowmobile engines reverberated in her ears, and the blinding white settled on her face. A sour-tasting rush of panic filled Teddi's mouth as her pulse thundered.

Without realizing it, she clamped her mittened fingers on Grant's arms as the next hill flew toward them. She forced herself to stare at it with wide eyes and felt the ache in her throat, heard her heart hammering in her ears.

But this time she was prepared for the awful moment when the snow shot up around them and sprayed over her face. She drew a hard, deep breath and held it as the snowmobile smashed over the top.

At the bottom of the hill, Grant spun the snowmobile to a halt and turned to look at her. "Okay?" he asked gently, staring into her white face.

Teddi answered through clenched teeth. "Again. Do it again." Her heart was pounding so loudly she thought he must hear it.

Grant smiled at her, then kissed her cheek. His gloves gripped the wheel, and he stepped on the accelerator. The next hill rushed forward, filling Teddi's vision. She sat back and clamped her fingers on the edges of the seat, clenched her teeth and waited.

The snowmobile shot over the top and seemed to hang suspended in a haze of flying snow; then the runners touched the snowpack and glided forward. Teddi slowly released her breath and wiped the melting crystals from her face.

An exhilarated smile illuminated her face. "I did it," she breathed. She pounded Grant's shoulder with her fist, excitement dancing in her eyes. "Again. Let's do it again!"

Teddi threw back her head and laughed up at the sun sparkling through the blizzard of flying snow. It was all right. It was better than all right; it was wonderful! The sun and the scent of spruce and the glistening snow and the cold plumes of air frosting her breath—it was glorious, fabulous, intoxicating!

She was almost disappointed when the moguls lay in the distance behind them. Then the snowmobiles crossed each other's tracks, playing a crazy game of Keystone Kops, and Teddi laughed and threw snowballs with the others and felt like a teenager again.

When they reached Buck and Judy's ranch, they parked the snowmobiles, and Kelly pointed to a drift of snow nearly as tall as she was. "Hey, Teddi. Remember?"

Turning, Kelly spread out her arms and fell flat against the snowdrift. She moved her arms and legs, then stood and looked down at the impression she'd made.

"Angels," Teddi laughed. Delighted, and feeling reckless with triumph, she fell into the snowdrift and waved her arms and feet. For an instant the sudden shock of cold against her back caught her breath. Then she was laughing and reaching for Grant to pull her to her feet. "Your turn," she said, pushing him into the snowdrift. Then everyone had to do it.

When they trudged into Buck and Judy's house to change into swimming suits for the hot tub, a row of smudged snow angels stamped the drift as theirs.

Buck made wine spritzers, and Grant served them; then they ran through the snow toward the steam rising off the hot tub, laughing and screaming as their bare feet sank in the snow.

"This," Judy said when they were cozied into the tub, sipping the spritzers and ignoring the drifts piled beside the path, "is the life. Good friends, good wine and a hot tub."

They all agreed. Teddi found Grant's toes beneath the water and raised her glass to him in a silent toast. He grinned at her through the steam and lifted his wine. "To the Sterling Four-Day-Wonder Plan."

"What on earth is that?" Kelly asked.

Buck rolled his eyes toward the cold clear sky. "As if we can't guess."

Teddi grinned and splashed hot water over his smile. "Well, you're wrong."

"It wouldn't be the first time," Judy interjected after a glance at Teddi's bright cheeks. Tactfully, she changed the subject, teasing Buck about a domestic mix-up. Kelly joined with a story of her own that Jim protested, and the conversation turned lively.

Teddi looked at Grant, and her heart expanded. The wind had chapped his cheeks to a healthy pink beneath his tan. And when he laughed, his teeth flashed strong and white. She longed to brush his damp hair back from his forehead. Suddenly she realized he was studying her as intently as she was studying him. And she sensed that his thoughts, too, had jumped ahead to tonight.

Beneath the water, his foot found hers and moved suggestively up her calf. She stared at him through soft eyes and wet her lips in a provocative gesture.

"Young love!" Kelly laughed. Jim grinned and tightened his arms around her shoulders.

"Don't tell me the last bastion of bachelorhood is about to crumble," Buck groaned.

"WERE WE THAT TRANSPARENT?" Teddi asked as Grant parked the Mercedes and opened the door for her.

"Do you care?" Grant murmured, kissing her throat.

She gazed at him in the dim light of the new moon and smiled. "Right now the only thing I care about is you."

"If you don't make love to me in the next two minutes, I'm going to go crazy. All through dinner the only thing I could think of was how fabulous you looked in that bikini.''

"You didn't look so bad yourself, Sterling."

He patted her on the fanny, then chased her up the stairs and inside the house. Teddi flung off her cap and parka and dashed up the stairs to his bedroom, laughing over her shoulder.

Grant grabbed her, and they fell across the quilt. In a moment he had her pinned and was staring down at her face, lit by the faint moonlight streaming through the skylight.

Teddi gazed into the mounting desire transforming his eyes into smoldering points of golden brown. She lifted trembling fingertips and smoothed his hair back from his temples.

"You smell like snow and mountain air and something sweet and feminine," Grant said in a thick voice.

Smiling against his lips, Teddi closed her eyes and surrendered to the solid warmth of his body covering her own. "Are you going to build a fire?"

"Right now."

Then he was kissing her with an exciting blend of passion and slow deliberation. First Teddi felt weak at the onslaught of his lips and hands; then her body ignited, and she strained against him, wanting to melt into him and become a part of all that was Grant Sterling.

Despite the pounding urgency, Teddi made herself follow the lazy pace Grant established. Slowly he drew her sweater over her head, then her turtleneck. She drew a finger down his muscled chest as she unbuttoned his shirt, teasing him with her lips and fingertips.

Finally, they were both naked, lying side by side on the bed, not touching but staring deeply into each other's eyes.

"Teddi, I . . ."

Afraid of what he might be about to say, Teddi covered his mouth with a lingering, exploring kiss. As the kiss deepened, he drew her roughly into his arms, and she gasped as she felt the hard strength of his desire against her thighs. A light moisture broke over her skin, giving it a dewy look of satin in the moonlight, and she felt a flood of liquid heat rush toward her center.

All thought spun from her mind as a tidal flow of sensation overwhelmed her. Grant's hands gently cupped her arching breasts, molding them in his large hands. His kisses trailed over her throat, behind her ear, discovered the sensitive area near her hard nipples. His mouth moved lower, igniting flames of tension across her stomach, her inner thighs, and finally, when she thought she would explode, his tongue flicked at the core of her desire and Teddi smothered a small scream of exquisite pleasure.

Her fingers clawed into his shoulders, and her head arched back against the pillow. She called his name, pleading to be fulfilled. Finally, when the tension and the waves of pleasure were so intense as to be almost painful, Grant allowed her the release she begged for.

When her labored breath returned to normal, Teddi turned in his arms. She kissed the pulse beat at the hollow of his throat, then teased her tongue in circles around his nipples, pleased by his low groan. Her hands slid down his torso and traced a path to a tapering waist and the slight flare of his hips. Slowly, slowly, tantalizing him as he had tantalized her, she covered his body with fiery darting kisses until she gave him the same release he had given her.

Later, they made love again. Teddi thought the urgency had been appeased, but the moment he lifted above her and her long legs wrapped around him, she knew their passion was as intense as it had been an hour ago.

"I can't get enough of you," Grant whispered against her damp hair.

"I know," she said. "I know." Her arms tightened around his neck, and she surrendered to their rhythm. Never had she felt this warm and cherished and fulfilled. Each time was better than the last; each time she discovered something new in their lovemaking. And it was wonderful.

"Teddi?" he murmured drowsily against the back of her neck.

"Hmm?"

"Tomorrow we'll ski the beginner slopes."

Teddi's eyes flared open in the darkness, and her body stiffened.

"Okay?"

"I..." Suddenly her mouth was dry. "I think we should talk about it."

But he was asleep, his breathing slow and regular. Teddi stared blindly at the bar of moonlight creeping across the oak floor. She suspected she needn't worry about snoring tonight. The prospect of skiing had wiped all thought of sleep from her mind.

Chapter Nine

Sometime before dawn Teddi slipped from the bed and tiptoed into the bathroom. As she couldn't sleep, she decided she might as well get dressed. She went downstairs to the kitchen and put on a fresh pot of coffee.

When the coffee was brewed, she sat at the table, cradling a cup in her hands and staring past the windows at Nichol Run. Gradually, the blue shadows darkening the slope faded to golden pink.

She didn't want to ski.

Skiing would fling wide the last door to the past. It would all be there before her. Unfinished business. The minute she snapped on her binders, she would have to ask herself if she could still beat the mountain. And if she could, then she would have to question if she could have placed at Lake Placid. And that question could never be answered. It was too late. The opportunity was gone, just as Peter and Kip were gone.

A sparkle of tears hung on her lashes. If only she could turn back the clock and relive that day, the day that had irrevocably changed her life. This time she would insist they avoid Pine Overhang; they would leave an hour earlier or an hour later. Somehow she would make the day end differently, and then everything would be all right.

Teddi bit her lip and stared into the coffee cup as her shoulders slumped. Her father had asked if she had regrets, and she'd murmured a vague reply. But she had regrets; oh, yes. All her life she would wonder what might have happened at Lake Placid if she'd been there. She'd wonder how Peter's life would have unfolded and if she and Kip could have been happy together.

With a flash of insight, Teddi realized she was worrying the past like a dog with an old bone. Going over it again and again long after there was anything to be gained.

She was avoiding the current problem. Skiing today.

She couldn't do it. She didn't want to do it.

She tried to think of an excuse to offer Grant as to why she couldn't ski with him. She had no valid reason except "I can't." And that, she knew, he wouldn't accept.

In the end, the reasons didn't matter. What mattered was that she dreaded skiing with an intensity that erupted in nervous perspiration and tightened her nerves until her fingers trembled. If she tried to ski when she was this tense, she was setting herself up for a serious accident. At the very least, she'd make a fool of herself.

Realizing she'd reached a decision, she got to her feet. Relief flooded Teddi's features as she dialed for a taxi, followed by an uncomfortable rush of self-dislike as she penned a hasty note to Grant telling him she was needed at the Edelweiss today.

Slipping outside, Teddi waited by the road for the taxi, breathing the icy morning air and fighting waves of guilt.

TEDDI'S PARENTS smiled with pleasure when Teddi entered the dining room and joined them for breakfast. After a quick glance behind Teddi, Marta's eyebrows rose. "Where's Grant?"

Pointedly ignoring her mother's question, Teddi pretended to study the menu. She cleared her throat. "I think it's time I went home," she announced quietly.

Hans looked confused. "But you are home."

"I meant Lahaina. It's been wonderful seeing you both, and I've had a good time, but..." There was no way to explain what she was feeling. "But it's time I went home," she finished, knowing the explanation, such as it was, was inadequate.

Hans and Marta looked at each other, then at Teddi. "Have we done or said something to upset you?" Hans asked.

"No! It's nothing like that." *Oh, Lord,* Teddi thought dismally. "You know how it is in the hotel business," she said, hating having to deceive them. "I'm starting to worry about the Alii, about the new cook and the cleaning crew, about whether or not the reservations are holding up for the Christmas season." Her gaze begged for understanding. "You know."

The pleasure faded from their eyes, replaced by resignation. Hans nodded. "We understand," he said finally.

"When will you be leaving?" her mother asked.

Aching inside, Teddi raised her coffee cup with shaking hands. "Tomorrow. If I can change my reservations." The next words emerged in an unplanned tumble. "I—I'm thinking about taking over the Edelweiss. I just haven't made up my mind yet."

Her father reached to stroke her hair. "Don't worry about it, Theodora. Your mother and I talked it over. We don't have any right to pressure you. We just thought it would be nice if—"

A shrill note entered Teddi's voice. "Please. I just need more time to think about it. Okay?"

"Of course, darling," her mother said. "There's no hurry at all." She peered into Teddi's pale face.

"We don't want you to do anything that isn't right for you."

But what was right? Teddi didn't know anymore. She only knew that she experienced a deep longing for her beach house in Lahaina, for a life where she wasn't assaulted by guilt and anxiety wherever she turned.

After breakfast, she called the airline and arranged a noon flight for tomorrow. Then she went to her room to pack. When she finished, she sank into the rocker by the window and stared at her trophies. Once they had filled her with pride; now they seemed to taunt her. Sighing, she shifted her gaze to the window and looked out at the drifts edging the parking lot. And she felt like burying her head in her hands and surrendering to a storm of weeping.

EVERY TIME the phone rang Teddi started and glanced up from the registration counter, expecting it to be Grant. But he didn't call. As the long day dragged toward dinner, she gradually accepted that he wasn't going to phone. The tight ache in her chest indicated it wasn't relief she was feeling but disappointment.

When she saw him emerge from the staircase leading to the shops downstairs, her heart stopped, then raced. She watched as he approached the counter, stopping to speak to Marta.

As always, he walked tall, as if the world were his for the taking, and he carried his cane, swinging it lightly by his side. A tweed jacket covered a cream-colored sweater. Teddi looked at him with her heart in her eyes, then turned aside and tried to think what she would say to him.

"Grant, wait." Marta intercepted him by placing her hand on his sleeve. She examined his face, then added quietly, "You're angry."

Was he? Perhaps. But more than that, he was disappointed and frustrated. He'd been so certain Teddi was ready to ski again. She'd done so well with the snowmobiling. Then he'd awakened to her note and had immediately seen through her excuses. She wasn't willing to try.

"A little," he admitted, looking toward the registration counter. Teddi avoided his glance. When he looked back at Marta, he thought she looked tired, discouraged. He covered her hand, and his face softened. "Are you resting in the afternoons?"

She waved aside the question. "When there's time. Grant...Teddi's leaving tomorrow. Going back to Maui."

His eyes widened, then narrowed, and his mouth set. Damn. If only he'd had a little more time. He looked across the lodge and wondered if he wanted the time for Hans and Marta or for himself. Hell, who was he trying to kid? He wanted her at the Edelweiss as much for himself as for the Ansels.

"I'm sorry," he said softly. Marta bit her lip and stared at a point over his shoulder. "Tell her, Marta. Or allow me to."

Marta shook her head. "No. But thank you, Grant. We know you tried to help."

But it hadn't been enough, obviously. Teddi was following the pattern she'd established years ago. He wanted to shake her until she realized that. Mouth grim, he approached the counter.

"We need to talk, Teddi. Can you get away?"

Teddi winced at the uncompromising flatness in his tone. She glanced up from the key bucket and looked a question at Marta, who waved a plump hand and said easily, "I can manage. You two run along."

Wordlessly, Teddi followed to the chairs facing the lodge fireplace. She sank into a chair and clasped her hands in her lap.

"Okay, Teddi. What's this all about? I thought you agreed to work out the problem areas."

"I'm going home tomorrow, Grant." She made herself meet his gaze.

"So Marta tells me. Are you that afraid of skiing again?"

"What's the point?" She sounded defensive and hated it. "My life is in Maui."

Grant stared at her. "You're running away."

Irritation flashed across Teddi's blue eyes. "No, I'm going home. This was a vacation, remember?

People go home after vacations." His silence was like an accusation, and it made her angry and defensive.

"I thought you said you couldn't have a future until you beat the past."

"No, Grant, that's what *you* said." Suddenly, Teddi felt weary to the point of exhaustion. "I made a mistake. I agreed to the Sterling Plan for the wrong reasons. I agreed because I wanted to please you. But that isn't enough of a reason."

"No, it isn't." He leaned forward, his hands clasped over the curve of his cane. "You have to fight your own ghosts, Teddi, because *you* want to." His golden stare pinned her in place. "Are you telling me you don't want to face the past?"

She wet her lips and clenched her hands. "I'm telling you that it's my life. That I have to please me, not you or anyone else." Her chin firmed in a stubborn line.

Grant nodded slowly. "I agree. What I don't understand is why it pleases you to run away."

"I'm *not* running away, dammit! I've overcome a lot of emotional obstacles during my vacation, Grant, and I appreciate your advice and help. But my life is in Maui. I need to go back, I need to see how the new, guiltless Teddi fits in."

They stared at each other across the small space separating them. Then Grant stood and looked down at her. "Do you need a ride to Denver?"

"No, I'm taking the bus. It's faster and easier."

She looked up at him, knowing her knees wouldn't support her if she attempted to stand. It was over. Whatever small beginning they had made was ending, and she felt powerless to prevent it. Hurting inside, she stared at him, at the strength in his face and stance. And she wanted to fling herself into his arms and hold on forever.

"I love you, Teddi."

Suddenly tears blinded her. Why did he choose this moment to reveal the depth of his feelings? It would only make her decision harder to follow through. But she had to. Fighting to keep her voice steady, she whispered, "I'm not the tough lady you want, Grant."

"You're plenty tough, Ansel. Give yourself a chance and discover just how tough you are. Not for my sake but for yours."

"I can't."

"The hell you can't." He spat the words. His face was set in a mask of determination, of strength. Without a waver in his voice, he accused her. "You won't."

She looked up at him, her eyes flashing through the glitter of tears. "All right, Grant. I won't. I don't want to. So where does that leave us?"

"Right where we started. You're running away from Hans and Marta and the Edelweiss, you're running away from me, and most important, you're running away from yourself."

Teddi's fingers clamped on the arms of the chair. "So that's it. The end."

"Not a chance, Ansel." A ghost of a grin brushed his lips. "I'm not a quitter. I don't give up, remember?" The smile faded, and his fiery eyes swept her body. "This is a hiatus, that's all. A time for you to think about what's important."

Teddi shook her head. "I know what's important."

"Think about it."

She watched him across the lodge, pause to speak to Marta and then descend the staircase. "I love you," she whispered, testing the words on her tongue. Then she fell forward and buried her face in trembling hands. "I love you." And it hurt. It hurt badly.

SHE FELT NO BETTER when she boarded the bus for Denver and Stapleton Airport. Leaning out the window, she waved and blew kisses to her parents, who stood in the snow looking up at her. It was bitterly cold, and the slate-colored sky promised more snow. "I love you," she said silently, mouthing the words.

"We love you, too," Marta said in reply. A silvery plume of frost hung in the air in front of her lips.

Then the bus was pulling away, and in moments Marta's red coat and Hans's blue parka were lost to view. Teddi straightened in her seat and bit her thumbnail and tried to spot Grant's house among those perched on the side of the mountains.

And she asked herself why she was doing this. Did she genuinely love her job and her life in Lahaina as she'd thought? Or was she running away as Grant had suggested? Suddenly, the question no longer involved snow and cold but centered on Maui. Why *was* she living there?

Teddi touched her fingertips to her temples. Damn Grant Sterling, anyway! She'd come home seeking answers and because of him had ended with more questions. And with a strange emptiness that ached inside.

Chapter Ten

Christmas in Lahaina was a festive event. Each year the town council draped the banyan tree beside the courthouse with twinkling lights, sponsored carolers who strolled along the wharf and Front Street, and gleefully reported the holiday blizzards that closed mainland airports from Maine to Utah. All the major hotels arranged Christmas Eve luaus, and the Alii was no exception.

After checking with the cook to be certain the pig roasting in the sand pit would be fully cooked by the time the hotel dancers finished their show, Teddi relaxed against the trunk of a royal palm and absently watched her friend Carol Kokuna swiveling her hips in a Yuletide hula.

A light breeze blowing off the ocean ruffled Teddi's hair around her shoulders and freshened the scent of the ginger blossom tucked behind her ear. Sighing, she tasted her Mai Tai and tilted her head toward the stars.

She'd been back three and half weeks now, long enough that Vail should have faded from her memory. But it hadn't. If anything, thoughts of home were stronger now than at any time in the past.

Vail was enjoying a white Christmas—she'd seen the news on the television "Home Report." The village would twinkle with tiny lights, looking like a snow-frosted vision from a fairy tale. Every year her father helped erect a huge pine tree in the village square, and Teddi could envision it behind her eyelids. She could almost see the lights flashing through the snow, could imagine she felt tiny snowflakes melting on her lashes.

"Merry Christmas."

Teddi started, then smiled guiltily at Carol. "Finished already?"

Laughing, Carol accepted a Mai Tai from a passing waiter. "Where have you been? The show ran long tonight." She tossed back waves of thick black hair and leaned to study Teddi in the light of the leaping tiki torches. "Hey, Scrooge, it's Christmas Eve, remember? What's with the bah-humbug expression?"

"I don't know." Teddi gazed at the waves rolling toward the beach. Warm air bathed her bare shoulders. "I miss the snow. There ought to be snow for Christmas."

"You're kidding. Look around you, Theodora Ansel. All these people paid a small fortune to escape the snow you're mooning around about." She gestured for Teddi to follow as she headed toward the hotel to change out of her costume.

In the dancer's dressing room, Teddi looked at herself in the mirror as Carol wriggled out of her grass skirt and stepped into a muumuu. "I look terrible," Teddi said.

"Oh, brother. I should look so terrible." Carol raised an eyebrow. "When someone as gorgeous as you starts thinking she looks terrible, there's a man in the picture. Right?"

Teddi stared at the gold hair curling on her bare shoulders, at the bright red-and-green sarong gently molding her breasts before dropping to her sandals. Outwardly she looked lovely. But the spark from within was missing.

"If you mean Grant, why don't you just say so," she responded irritably. "I'm beginning to wish I'd never told you about him."

Unperturbed, Carol leaned in to the mirror to apply fresh lipstick. "Well? What are you going to do about him?"

"If you ask me that one more time, I'm going to scream."

"There's something the ancient kahunas used to say that you should give some thought to: 'Each person is guaranteed happiness.'"

Teddi eyed Carol suspiciously. Part of Carol's charm rested in her propensity to invent an old kahuna saying for every occasion. "Oh? And how does anyone guarantee happiness, pray tell? Did your ancestors explain that part?"

Carol smiled. "Sure. Only you know what it takes to make you happy. And only you can make the changes it takes to have that happiness. Therefore, if you're willing to make the changes, you're—"

"Guaranteed happiness," Teddi finished. She made a face.

"Right. So how badly do you want Grant Sterling?" She laughed at Teddi's expression, her dark eyes crinkling into an almond shape. "Come on. Isn't the boss lady supposed to be out there mingling with the tourists? I, for one, am starving."

When they were seated around the mats spread over the sand, sampling the feast served on fresh palm leaves, Teddi leaned to Carol's ear. "Did you make all that up? About the kahuna and happiness?"

Carol met her friend's eyes. "Does it matter?" she asked gently. "Teddi, you've been moping around since you returned. I'd be less than a friend if I didn't point out that you need to make a decision. Forget him, or go get him."

Teddi bit her lip. "Well," she said brightly. "Are we meeting at the Broiler when this shindig is over?'' Years ago, she and her friends had established a tradition of celebrating Christmas Eve on the outdoor patio of the Lahaina Broiler. But as soon as the question popped from her mouth, she realized she didn't want to go this year.

When the luau ended, she murmured hasty excuses to Carol and escaped before Carol could ask any of the questions Teddi saw in her eyes.

Instead, she drove to her house and changed into a terry robe and thongs, then made herself a cup of eggnog and sat on the sofa, watching the lights strung around her plastic tree blink on and off.

Suddenly Teddi realized she hated plastic Christmas trees. They had no scent, they were too perfectly formed, and they were offensive to the spirit. Quickly finishing her eggnog, she turned her back to the tree and reached for her gifts.

When she'd reduced the stack of presents to one, she drew a long breath and fortified herself with another eggnogg. Slowly she opened the last card: ''Missing you. Love, Grant.'' After placing the card to one side, she pulled open the ribbon tying his gift and pushed back layers of gaily colored wrapping paper.

He'd sent her a ski sweater. A thick hand-knit sweater made from expensive Irish wool. Teddi stared at it, then burst into laughter.

It was seventy-two degrees outside, and a warm night breeze flirted with the open draperies. But if a sudden blizzard blew over the islands and the temperature dropped below freezing, she was ready. Shaking her head, she folded the sweater across her lap and thought about him. She hoped he liked the cane she'd sent. She'd found one carved from driftwood and fitted with a scrimshaw crook. It had been more expensive than she'd planned for, but once she saw it, she'd wanted him to have it.

Closing her eyes, Teddi pushed the wrapping paper off the coffee table and crossed her ankles, leaning back with a long sigh. What was Grant doing tonight? Was he at the lodge with Marta and Hans? Or in the square, singing carols around the tree?

When she could no longer bear the sight of the plastic Christmas tree, Teddi unplugged the lights and went to bed. It was the most miserable Christmas she'd ever spent.

"TELEPHONE, Miss Ansel."

Teddi looked up from the registration desk with a hint of annoyance in her eyes. "I told you no calls, Tiko. Just take a message and I'll get back to everyone when I finish straightening out this mess." The hotel was overbooked, which was always a nasty problem. New accommodations would have to be arranged, and the Alii would absorb any difference in cost. It was an unjustified expense and as such would cut into Teddi's year-end bonus.

"This is the third time Miss Kokuna has telephoned." Tiko looked at her uncertainly, his black eyes questioning.

"Oh, all right." Listening to the staccato tap of her heels, Teddi walked to the phone and lifted the receiver. "Carol? This better be important."

Carol's voice was slightly breathless. "You tell me. Is this important? Tall, reddish-brown hair, wide shoulders, a dark tan, and he's carrying a cane. And Teddi, this guy is gorgeous!"

Teddi's heart stopped. "Carol, what are you talking about?"

"I stopped in at Moira's Gallery. Remember that painting I was telling you about?"

"Carol . . ."

"Okay, never mind the painting. This absolutely fabulous man comes into the gallery, carrying the cane you bought before Christmas, by the way, and he asked Moira how to find the Royal Alii. So, very casually, I say, 'Do you happen to be from Colorado?' And he said . . ."

As if in a trance, Teddi muttered something into the phone, then hung up. For an instant she couldn't think, couldn't move.

Then a dozen thoughts crowded her mind at once. She had to do something with her hair. And she hadn't yet okayed the menu for tonight's banquet. Grant was here? In Lahaina? There were still four people to place at another hotel, and she had to interview the girl from the Liscet Agency. Could it be true? Was he really here? Carol had never met Grant; she could easily be mistaken.

Hurrying to the desk, Teddi hastily swung the reservation ledger around to face her. She found his name immediately. Grant Sterling; Vail, Colorado. "When did this come in?" she asked sharply.

The reservations clerk looked at her, then at the ledger. "The day after Christmas, Miss Ansel."

"Do I look all right?"

The man's eyebrows soared toward his hairline. "You look beautiful, Miss Ansel," he blurted out.

Teddi bit her tongue. "Thank you," she muttered stiffly, feeling heat flood her cheeks. She was behaving like an idiot.

Looking down, she smoothed her hands over the slim skirt of her suit, glad she'd chosen her blue silk instead of a loose-fitting muumuu. Quickly she lifted her fingertips to her hair and tucked an errant strand behind the gardenia pinned above her ear.

She saw him at the same moment Grant saw her. Heart accelerating, she stood as if rooted in place and watched him cross the lobby toward her. Her mouth dried, and butterflies fluttered in her stomach. She had promised herself that no man could be as handsome as she remembered him. But he was. He wore an off-white linen jacket above chocolate slacks, an open-collared silk shirt and no tie. It wasn't just the cane at his side that turned people's heads; it was the presence he possessed, that indefinable something that surrounded him like an aura.

He stopped a few feet from Teddi, close enough that she felt his body heat and inhaled the familiar musk of his after-shave. "We've got to stop meeting like this," he said, smiling down into her wide eyes. "One hotel lobby after another. What will people think?"

"What are you doing here? Why didn't you tell me you were coming?"

His smile widened into a grin. "It's nice to see you, too. And yes, I had an interesting flight. No, I'm not tired. But yes, I am hungry."

Teddi laughed and made a flustered gesture with her hands. Then she gazed into his smile, and her eyes softened. "I'm glad to see you." It was more than that. She felt ecstatic, vividly alive, as she hadn't been since she'd returned to Lahaina. "It's been six weeks," she blurted out feeling a rush of color warm her cheeks.

"Six endlessly long weeks," Grant Sterling stared down into her eyes, and Teddi caught her breath at his smoldering appraisal. "You're more beautiful than I remembered," he said gruffly. "I didn't think that was possible."

He didn't kiss her, didn't touch her, but Teddi felt his strength enfold her, felt the fluttery tension of his nearness. She gazed up at him and listened to her pulse pounding in her ears, felt her knees go weak. She tried to speak, but no sound emerged.

As if he knew exactly what was happening to her, Grant smiled and lifted a thick eyebrow. "Are you going to point me toward registration? Or leave me standing here in the middle of the lobby?"

Registration. It was a buzzword that returned Teddi to a semblance of professional demeanor. Her thoughts swirled, then settled down. An impish smile illuminiated her face. "There's a slight problem with registration, Mr. Sterling. Unfortunately the hotel is overbooked." She raised a hand. "But don't worry. I will personally arrange alternate accommodations." Her eyes lingered on his wide, firm mouth, and her voice dropped to a throaty register. "I think you'll like them."

He stared at her lips. "I think so, too."

"If you'll wait in the lounge for, say, fifteen minutes, I have a few things to do here, then I'll show you to your rooms."

Grant's hand lifted, and for a moment Teddi thought he would stroke her cheek. She held her breath, waiting for the rush of electricity to shoot through her body. But he touched the gardenia instead. "Lovely." The heat of his hand radiated against her skin, and for an instant she felt dizzy and light-headed.

They looked into each other's eyes; then Teddi swallowed hard and turned aside before she abandoned all effort to appear professional and threw herself into his arms. "Fifteen minutes," she repeated weakly.

It was closer to thirty minutes before she accomplished everything required to free her afternoon. But when she collected Grant and his luggage, she left the Alii confident that the assistant manager could handle all the loose ends.

She drove out of the Alii parking lot and past manicured grounds. Turning right, toward Lahaina, she fought to believe he was actually here. "Why didn't you tell me you were coming?"

"Because I wasn't sure you'd welcome me if you knew why I'm here." One finger stroked the back of her neck and played with the wisps of golden hair curling along her collar.

Teddi shivered and gripped the wheel. "Why are you here?"

"Two reasons. First, I want to thank you for the cane." It lay between them on the car seat.

Teddi smiled. "You could have accomplished that with a note."

"And I'm here to put as much pressure on you as I can." She turned to stare at him. "I want you to come home, Teddi. And Hans and Marta want you to come home."

"Well," she said after a moment, "at least you're up front about it." When he started to add something, she cut him off. "But I don't think you'll succeed." The lightness in her tone didn't reflect what she was feeling. "Look around you— this is heaven."

Sparkling blue waves rolled up white beaches. Palms trees waved lazily along the road. To their left, fields of deep green sugarcane climbed the mountainside. And when she guided the Lincoln Continental onto Front Street, crowded with smiling tourists, the shorts and halter tops underscored the soft balmy sunshine.

Teddi smiled sweetly and blinked large innocent eyes. "What was the weather when you left?"

"Now, why do I have the impression you already know?" He grinned at her and gently tugged the strand of hair curling around his fingertip. "Six degrees and snowing. A beautiful day."

Laughing, Teddi eased the car through traffic, then grabbed a rare vacant parking slot near the courthouse, which faced the wharf. "This is the heart of Lahaina," she said grandly. A forest of masts rocked at the dock in front of the courthouse. Behind the building one of the world's largest banyan trees spread its shady limbs over two-thirds of an acre. "It's over a hundred years old," Teddi explained proudly. "Sooner or later, everyone shows up here, to sit in the shade, exchange gossip and catch up with whatever's going on.''

She knew she was babbling but couldn't stop herself. ''The historical society has preserved the old jail in the basement of the courthouse—you'll want to see that. And if you want to fish or dive, you can make arrangements at that booth on the wharf. See it?''

''Teddi . . .''

''Before the Pioneer Hotel was built, King Kamehameha III had his royal taro patch and fish ponds right about here, and—''

''Teddi.''

''Lahaina began as a whaling village back in missionary times. Between November and May you can usually see the humpbacks from any shore road. They—''

''Teddi, stop.''

She looked at him and drew a long deep breath.

''I love you,'' he said quietly.

Teddi gazed at him helplessly. ''Oh, Grant. I've missed you so much.'' Her voice emerged in a whisper. By not touching, they had created a tension between them that was tangible. It quivered and shimmered and drew Teddi's nerves as taut as wire. Her stomach alternated between periods of fluttery elation and knotted urgency.

Now Grant's fingertips brushed her cheek, and his light touch left her breathless. "Let's go home," he said hoarsely.

"Yes," she whispered, staring into his eyes.

Neither of them spoke as she drove the short remaining distance to her beach house. Small, but adequate for one person, it was surrounded by lush tropical growth. Large windows faced a strip of private beach and flooded the interior with mellow soft light.

"This is it," Teddi said, leading him inside. A quiet pride infused her expression. The house was small, but white wicker furniture upholstered in bright greens and yellows made the space appear larger. The walls were a muted green hung with the artwork she'd collected since her arrival five years ago. Her intent had been to surround herself with casual comfort, to create an environment that was both relaxing and welcoming.

Grant scarcely noticed. He stood in her living room, dominating the space, and stared at her, naked hunger in his eyes.

Then his large warm hands framed her face. For a long moment he examined her wide helpless eyes; then his mouth slowly descended to hers. He kissed her gently at first; then, as Teddi parted her lips and wrapped her arms around his neck, his kiss deepened with mounting passion.

When he finally released her, they were both breathing heavily, and Teddi was trembling. Swaying on her feet, she stepped out of her heels, her eyes never leaving his, and slowly she dropped her silk jacket to the floor and her shaking fingers rose to the buttons on her blouse.

Grant dropped his jacket across the back of a chair, and then his shirt. He made a low sound in the back of his throat as Teddi's blouse parted to reveal the creamy lace underneath. Catching her in his arms, he kissed her deeply, urgently, and his hands molded her body in long, exploratory strokes.

Moaning softly, Teddi broke away, and taking his hand, she led him down a short hallway and into the cool shadows of her bedroom. There her fingers fumbled with the button on her skirt, and she watched as he stepped from his slacks, then lay on the bed and opened his arms to her.

With a low cry, she came to him, bending over him and showering his face with kisses. A thousand times she had imagined him here, his russet curls on her pillow, the long, hard length of him stretched across her bed.

Rising slightly, Grant flicked his tongue across her nipples as they rose in taut readiness. He would have teased her further, but Teddi covered his mouth with a fiery kiss that told him her passion was already at a peak that precluded further play.

When his weight covered her, she closed her eyes and knew this was what she had craved in the long, lonely hours since her return. Grant Sterling. Her long tanned body opened to him like a flower unfolding, urging him with a haste her frantic desire demanded.

When they had sated themselves with each other, they lay side by side, surrounded by the scent of crushed gardenia. Teddi found the flower that had fallen from her hair and laid it on the bedside table; then she shifted on her pillow to look into his strong face.

"I love you, Grant Sterling."

"Thank God." He kissed her chin, then smiled into her eyes. "I was beginning to think this was a one-sided commitment."

Yes, it was a commitment. One she hadn't planned to make. The words had slipped out without thought, because they were true and because her heart was too full not to give it expression.

"I love you," she repeated, her voice filled with wonder. She blinked at his grin. "How did this happen?"

"Ansel, you've got to be the least romantic woman I ever met. How did it happen? It happened because I am one terrific good deal. Because I'm charming and successful and have taken pity on you."

She laughed. "Taken pity on me?"

"Yes. A homely child like you." He grinned at the spill of silky hair fanning out around her face, at her slim curvaceous body, darkly tanned against the pale sheets. "It's gratitude you're feeling. You're happy as hell that some guy finally picked you up."

Laughing, she leaned forward and gently nipped his lower lip. "Gratitude, my Aunt Fanny. It's you who should be grateful that a bright, gorgeous girl like me gave you a second look."

"I am, I am." Smiling, he moved on top of her and kissed her lightly before the laughter faded, replaced by a slow, smoldering stare that swept her narrowed eyes and plundered her lips. "In fact," he said gruffly, "I think I should show you how grateful I am."

"Show me," Teddi whispered before his lips smothered further conversation.

THEY HAD DINNER at Longhis, stuffing themselves with Italian food and the most spectacular desserts on the island; then they strolled to the Blue Max for after-dinner drinks, choosing seats near the balcony railing to watch the sunset.

"Maui is famous for its sunsets," Teddi commented, intrigued by the play of orange and gold light across his face.

He played with her fingers across the table. "Marry me, Teddi."

Abruptly, the pleasure of the sunset fled her mind. "I—Grant, this is happening too fast."

He pressed her fingers within his palm. "I love you; you love me. Isn't marriage the next step?"

She forced a smile to her lips. "There are a few considerations in between, aren't there?"

"Such as?"

"Where we live, for one."

"In Vail," he answered promptly.

Teddi removed her fingers to stir her drink. "Why not here in Lahaina?" she asked softly.

"Because I have a substantial business investment in Colorado. And in case it's escaped your notice, there isn't much demand here for skiing and ski apparel."

His answer made sense. But she stubbornly persisted. "I have a job here, and a house."

"You can sell your house, and if you want to work, Hans and Marta have a job waiting for you at home. The Edelweiss is yours for the asking."

Teddi sighed. "Which brings us full circle, doesn't it?"

"Yes."

Lifting her face to the breeze off the ocean, Teddi transferred her gaze to the waves offshore, golden in the waning light. They were skirting the real issue: her refusal to come to terms with the past. It was one thing to speak of marriage here, far removed from memories of Kip and that last fatal day. But in Colorado... She shook her head to clear the sudden guilt that surged into her throat.

She raised a trembling hand to her eyes. "I do love you, Grant. But..."

"But?"

"But I need some time to think about this."

A frown creased his brow. "What is there to think about, Teddi? Either you've made a commitment or you haven't."

"It isn't that simple, and you know it. Please try to understand, Grant. Can't we go on like this for a while?"

"It isn't easy to maintain a satisfactory courtship when the people involved live thousands of miles apart."

"I know, but..." She shrugged helplessly. "You're asking more than marriage. You're asking a change of life-style."

He studied her in the pink-and-golden rays radiating from the ocean waves. "I'm asking you to share my life, Teddi."

"I love you, but I'm not sure I can love your life."

"You did once."

There was no satisfactory reply. Grant's life centered entirely on skiing—his business, his recreation, his residence. She felt the sensual Maui breezes on her skin and wondered if she could willingly trade them for snow and frigid cold. Or was that the true question? A tiny voice whispered in her ear, *Is Maui the life you really want? Or is it merely a refuge?*

When she didn't respond, Grant reached for her hand. "All right, think about it. Take as much time as you like as long as it's less than three days."

Her head snapped up. "Three days?"

"I'm leaving Monday."

"Can't you stay longer?" Dismay darkened her turquoise eyes to navy.

He smiled. "It doesn't take me long to say thanks for the cane, come home, and will you marry me."

"Three days," Teddi whispered. If she called the Alii first thing in the morning, she thought she could reschedule her duties to free the next three days. She didn't want to spend a single minute away from him.

"Have you decided yet?"

Teddi burst into laugher. "Sterling, you are absolutely relentless. Is this how it's going to be for the next three days?"

He nodded cheerfully. "Well?"

Her eyes sparkled mischievously. "I need some convincing."

His hands cupped her shoulders with rough warmth as he helped her to her feet. His lips brushed her temple. "I think I know just what you need."

Laughing, they ran hand in hand to Teddi's car.

Chapter Eleven

The narrow twisting road to Hana curved through lush tropical growth; ferns, ginger, wild violets and orchids brushed the sides of Teddi's car. Grant, who was driving, slowed to admire the extravagant beauty.

"Now this is how I pictured Maui," he said.

"This side of the island gets more rain."

"Which probably explains this rotten road." The route to Hana was pocked with deep potholes, wavy bumps in the tarmac, and was so narrow that oncoming traffic passed with difficulty.

Teddi laughed. "When we reach Hana, I'll buy you a T-shirt that reads: I survived the road to Hana."

He smiled at her, liking the relaxed sound of her laughter, the way dappled sunlight played through her hair. Today she wore hot pink shorts and a matching top that curved over her breasts and made it difficult for Grant to keep his mind on driving.

"Have you decided yet?"

"Not yet," Teddi answered, smiling.

After easing the car nearly off the road to facilitate the passage of an oncoming station wagon, Grant pretended to be crestfallen. "Well, when?"

Teddi's smile remained in place, but there was an undercurrent of anxiety in her voice. "What's the hurry?" she asked a bit too casually.

"Number one, I'm leaving soon. Number two, I'm an honorable fellow." When she tilted an eyebrow, he explained with a wink. "Someone should make an honest woman of you." She punched him on the arm and he grinned. "And three, we need to decide how many children we'll have."

"You want to decide how many children we'll have? Now?"

"I like to plan ahead."

Though he kept his tone light, he was curious how she felt about children. In Grant's mind, marriage was more than a melding of two people. Marriage was the root from which a family sprouted; a family fulfilled a marriage. Years ago he'd reached the realization that his only chance of experiencing a full family richness was to start one of his own. These thoughts had remained below the surface, quietly slumbering until he met Teddi. Now he found himself wondering what their children would look like. Would they have his russet hair or Teddi's silky blond? Would they be studious, or would they inherit their parents' athletic abilities? He smiled and shook his head. He was in love, all right. And it felt good. It would feel even better when she said the words he needed to hear.

"There's a waterfall up ahead you'll want a picture of."

"You're avoiding an answer, Ansel."

"Correct, Sterling."

After he'd dutifully snapped a photo of a spectacular waterfall, he helped Teddi back into the car, leering at her long tanned legs while she laughed.

"Now, about our children..." he said, easing the Lincoln onto the pitted road.

She frowned and looked out the window on the passenger side. Finally, she said, "I always imagined I'd have children if I married."

"Good. We're getting someplace."

"Grant..."

"We love each other, Teddi. The next step is marriage." He looked at the breeze teasing her hair through the open window and thought her the loveliest thing he'd seen. "Which brings up several issues we should discuss."

"I can see why you chose sales. You're a natural," she said, regarding him cautiously. "Is this an assumed close?"

He laughed. "Something like that. Assuming you know a good thing when you see it and agree to marry me—" she rolled her eyes and slid down the seat "—then we should discuss things like children and money and—"

"Where we live?" she interjected, the smile fading from her eyes.

It always came back to that. He pulled into a rare wide spot on the road and turned to face her. "Teddi, do you really think it's fair to ask me to sell out a sizable investment in Colorado?"

Her chin jutted slightly as she met his eyes. "Is it fair for you to ask me to sell my house and give up my job?"

"No," he said after a moment. "I suppose it isn't. But if we're to have a future, one of us must make some changes."

"Why does it seem to be me that's expected to make those changes?"

If he hadn't seen the anxiety behind her eyes, he might have made an issue of it. Sooner or later, she would have to look into herself and deal with the problems she'd left in Vail. She'd have to come to terms with "I can't." He gripped the steering wheel and told himself to go slowly with her. Except there wasn't time. When he'd planned this trip, he'd done so with the purpose of settling the loose ends between them. He wanted to know the direction of his own future. "I think you know why."

After an awkward silence, she touched his wrist. "Grant, please. Let's not spoil today."

"It's our future, Teddi."

"I know. But..." She spread her hands and wiped the perspiration-damp palms along the tops of her shorts. A deep breath didn't have the calming effect she'd hoped for. "I'm just not ready to talk about this."

"When will you be ready?"

"I...soon. All right? Soon."

He wanted to believe her. "All right, Teddi," he said, pulling out into the road. "Soon. Speaking of which, when do we get to Hana and that picnic you promised?"

Despite his easy change of subject Teddi sensed how much Grant needed her response and how much she continued to hurt him each time she refused him. Yet every time the subject of their future was brought up Teddi had the same unbidden reaction—fear. At the look in Grant's eyes, her heart went out to him.

"Grant. I do love you."

"I know," he said, smothering a sigh of frustration. That's what made her hesitation so difficult. He believed she loved him. It was in her eyes, in the warmth of her touch. She loved him, and he loved her. It should have been simple.

In a grassy meadow above Hana, Teddi spread a checkered cloth over the ground and laid out fried chicken, hard-boiled eggs and a wheel of cheese while Grant opened a bottle of Chablis chilled by the cooler.

Teddi waved a hand toward the ocean sparkling beyond the rooftops of Hana and grinned impishly. "How cold did you say it was in Vail?"

Laughing, he kissed her nose. "A sultry six degrees."

"And snowing?" She let the sea breeze catch her hair and spread it behind her like a ribbon of gold.

"And snowing." He cupped her face between his hands. "Perfect ski weather."

She met his steady gaze, then whispered, "Oh, Grant," and pressed her forehead against his shoulder.

Holding her, feeling her slight tremble against his body, Grant regretted the automatic response. He wasn't accustomed to taboo subjects, to sweeping topics beneath the carpet. Immediately, he grasped that much of what he said she would construe as pressure. But dammit, he wanted her to come home. To him. He wanted to wake up in the mornings with Teddi beside him, wanted to build a lifetime of memories with her, wanted to watch her hair turn silver. And he was beginning to understand it wouldn't happen unless something broke through to that part of her that was hidden away.

Tilting her face upward, he kissed her lightly, then stared into her eyes. "I'm sorry, Teddi. But we can't pretend my life doesn't exist." He traced the curve of her mouth with his thumb. "I love you. I've loved you from the moment I learned you hated chess and cards," he said, coaxing a small smile from her. "Now, are you going to feed me? Isn't that one of the tasks of an executive administrator?"

"Sounds more like a wifely task to me."

"You said it, not me."

They smiled at each other, and the awkwardness passed.

Later, when he'd helped Teddi pack away the remains of their picnic, they sat on the cloth, shoulders touching, enjoying the view, each other and the last of the wine.

"How are things at home? Are Mom and Dad all right?"

Instantly, the relaxed smile faded from Grant's lips, and he was glad Teddi couldn't see his face. He tightened his arm around her, guiding her head to his shoulder.

"They miss you," he said carefully.

"Pressure, pressure," she murmured, smiling into his collar.

"As you once pointed out, Hans and Marta are close to seventy..."

"And as you pointed out, what does their age have to do with anything?" Teddi pulled away from his shoulder and frowned into his eyes. "Is something wrong?"

He thought of Marta and the pills she carried in her apron pocket, thought of the worry in Hans's gaze when he looked at his wife. And he thought about the promise he'd made them. He felt like a man with his hands tied behind his back.

"They work too hard," he said finally, feeling the tenseness leave Teddi's shoulders as she leaned back into him.

"I know. I thought they looked tired when I was home. Especially Mom."

He'd never regretted a promise as much in his life. The urge to tell her about Marta's heart condition hovered on his tongue. Firmly, he reminded himself that as much as he loved the Ansels and thought of them as family, in actuality he was an outsider. He had no right to overturn Hans and Marta's decision.

"It's time they retired," he offered finally, his voice more grim than he'd intended.

The words were enough to galvanize Teddi. She jumped to her feet and dusted her hands, then looked at her watch. And he saw the color in her cheeks, the guilt in her eyes, and knew he'd put it there. He hadn't ignored the possibility, no, the certainty, of encountering touchy areas during his visit, and it wasn't his nature to avoid them. But he didn't want to hurt her. He only wanted to love her. Standing, he ran his gaze over her tanned legs and hot-pink shorts.

"This isn't exactly the way I pictured the end to this picnic," he said gruffly.

"What did you have in mind?" She teased.

"Come over here and I'll show you."

Smiling, she stepped into his arms; he spanned her waist with his hands, pulling her against his body and the sudden need he had for her. Soft lips opened beneath his, and he felt the full warmth of her breasts against his chest. Gently, they eased to their knees, still holding each other. And he tried to tell her with his mouth and hands how much he needed her, wanted her.

A burst of smothered giggles exploded above them.

Grant looked up the hill toward a clustered group of brownie scouts, hiding giggles behind small brown hands.

Teddi laughed and looked at him. "I think those young ladies are on a field trip."

He grinned at his audience, then at Teddi. "Two minutes more and they'd have had a lesson in anatomy." His gaze dropped to her lips, and he asked in a husky voice, "Has anyone made it down the Hana road in ten minutes flat?"

"We can try."

ONE OF THE THINGS he loved about Teddi was her competitive nature. He watched her sight down the fairway, then select a club with care and approach the tee, her concentration total. She looked like a pro when she swung.

"Damn."

"You pulled up on the downstroke."

"Did I ask for a critique, Sterling?"

He bowed from the waist and answered cheerfully. "No more than I did on the last hole. Turnabout is fair play."

She gave him a dark look that made him laugh; then they walked toward their balls, the caddies following. He swung his cane with a jaunty air, smiling when she made a face.

"David Nivenish, right?"

He grinned. "Right. Drives you ladies crazy with lust." He gave her a hopeful smile. "Tell me when you're overcome and I'll drag you under a palm tree."

Smiling, she pointed to his ball. "Did you come to play or to ogle me without even a token show of shame?"

"No contest. I'm here to ogle, leer and chase you around the course."

She laughed, then looked up at him with a softness in her eyes that made his stomach tighten. "Seriously, Grant. Is this too much walking for you? We could still send for a cart."

In truth, his leg ached, and he suspected she'd guessed as much. But a stubborn pride prevented him from giving in. Golf carts were too much like wheelchairs. "Am I slowing you down?" he asked, his voice lighter than he felt. Pride had also prevented him from wearing the brace today, for he was wearing shorts. He suspected he'd pay for this bit of foolishness with an aching stiffness for the next few days.

"Of course you're slowing me down. If it wasn't for you, I'd have eighteen holes in one and be back at the Alii clubhouse sipping a piña colada."

"Fat chance." He liked it that she didn't coddle him, didn't fuss over him or give quarter, yet she let him know she was concerned. There wasn't much about her that he didn't like. "Have you decided yet?"

"Make your shot, Sterling."

"Say you'll marry me, have three children and continue to wreck my golf scores for the rest of my life by wearing shorts like that."

She grinned up at him, and he wanted to kiss her. "Are you blaming your lousy score on my shorts?"

"What lousy score? I'm playing like Sam Sneed today."

"And I'm the Queen of Siam," she said after he'd made a less than perfect shot and was glaring toward the green.

"Well," he grumbled. "This isn't my sport."

"Oh? And what is?"

"Skiing." He said it without thinking, then cursed beneath his breath. After yesterday he'd sworn to go easy. But the problem was always there, like it or not. And it wasn't in his nature to dissemble. Fortunately, she didn't appear to notice, just nodded and smiled.

Later, over drinks, he looked at her glowing face and took her hand across the table. "Happy?"

"Yes, are you?"

Happier than he'd been in a long time. "Yes. This has been wonderful, Teddi."

But at the back of his mind was a shadow of doubt. What if she refused him? He could no longer imagine a life without her. But he reluctantly admitted the possibility existed. "What's next on the agenda?"

She gave him a teasing look. "I think a quiet evening at home." Her eyes grazed his mouth. "And tomorrow some heavy-duty sightseeing."

He pressed her hand, aware how hard she was trying to sell him on the benefits of living in Maui. "I like the idea of an evening at home."

"And tomorrow night I'm having a party for you."

"Sounds fine." But he wondered. He'd hoped to spend his last night alone with her. Was she afraid of the issues they'd left dangling? Of making the ultimate commitment? "I love you, Teddi."

He wished he had more confidence in what her decision would be even as he silently vowed tomorrow would be pressure-free. Grant stretched his leg and promised himself he wouldn't say another word about Vail until after her party. Unless she brought it up, which he didn't think she would.

Then he looked into her shining eyes and forgot even the ache in his leg. He loved her.

Chapter Twelve

Carol Kokuna propped her chin in her palm and gazed down the table at Grant. "I think I'm in love," she said sighing.

Teddi laughed and gazed proudly at Grant, who was talking to Jack and Sumi Morrison. It seemed to her that he looked particularly dashing and handsome tonight, but then, she admitted, she was wildly biased. Slipping from her seat, she removed the salad plates, then served her specialty, giant shrimp simmered in garlic-and-butter sauce.

"Perfect," Moira Emmerson murmured as her husband proposed a toast to Teddi and a dinner party that had been a success from the first moment.

Teddi blushed with pleasure and exchanged a look with Grant. It had been his suggestion to set the table on the lanai, where everyone would have a moonlit view of the ocean. Soft light from the flames in the tiki lamps illuminated Teddi's best linen and gleaming silver. She'd chosen ginger and plumeria for the centerpiece, and the fragrance spiced each breath. It was a perfect evening. The last evening, but she'd promised herself she wouldn't think about that.

"Tell me he has some terrible flaw," Carol continued when the conversation had picked up again. "I'll feel much better about him being crazy about you instead of me if I learn he's neurotic or boring or lousy in bed."

Teddi smiled. "If it will make you feel better, he's pushy, arrogant and tough as nails."

"The flaws, Teddi, tell me the flaws. Nothing you've said so far has done anything except make me salivate. I adore gorgeous, arrogant men who can be tough when they need to be."

Teddi looked at her friend. Tonight Carol wore a flowing caftan that enhanced her exotic beauty. Her thick black hair swung down her back. Leaning head to head, they made a striking pair. Teddi had chosen a form-fitting silk gown of a shade that nearly matched her eyes, and she'd brushed her golden hair to one side and caught it in a circle of scarlet blossoms.

"Carol, what am I going to do?" She gazed down the length of the table, and her heart filled to bursting. "I love him. But—but I don't fit into his life."

Carol tilted her head and squinted at the stars. "There's an old kahuna saying—"

"I thought there might be." Teddi smiled.

"'He who hesitates is lost.'" She gazed at Teddi from the corner of her eyes. "You think that's funny? Well, how about 'Life is what you make of it.'" She raised an eyebrow. "Okay, then, how's this: 'The perfect guy appears once in a lifetime, so jump on him.'"

"An old kahuna said that?" Teddi was choking on laughter.

"No, I said that. The old kahuna said aloha."

"Which means love—or farewell."

When Carol turned to her date, Teddi gazed at Grant. The last three days had been the most wonderful in her life. They had spent the morning sunning themselves on the beach, had explored parts of the island Teddi had always wanted to see, had played golf and had dived off the reef. And they had made love. Hot, urgent love and slow, lazy love; deliberate, teasing love and love that was wild and frenzied with passion.

She couldn't bear the thought that he was leaving in the morning. And she was no nearer a decision than she'd been the night of his arrival.

As with any successful party, the guests stayed later than Teddi had planned. It was nearly two when everyone departed.

"I like your friends, Teddi; they're nice people." They stood on the lanai, watching the taillights disappear toward town. "Is it true that an old kahuna once said, 'If she won't agree peaceably, take her by force?'"

Teddi laughed and nestled deeper into his arms. "Are you sleepy?"

"No. How about a walk?"

After changing into shorts and T-shirts, they strolled hand in hand along the shore, pausing when the moonlit surf bubbled up around their ankles.

A comfortable silence existed between them, unbroken until they reached the rock outcropping and turned back toward Teddi's house.

"It's time, Teddi," Grant said softly, squeezing her hand. "I need to know your decision."

Teddi had known the final moment was coming. And she'd dreaded it. After worrying her lower lip between her teeth, she drew a breath and returned the pressure against her fingers, looking up at him. "Why do we have to decide immediately?" she asked gently.

"I'm leaving in the morning."

"I know. But I thought maybe we could write and phone..." Her voice trailed off, and she felt a tightness in her throat. "You know, until we're sure that..."

"I'm sure. Very sure. Aren't you?"

"Yes, but..." A flutter of panic pulsed through her stomach, and she bit her lip hard. "I just..."

"Yes or no, Teddi."

They stood facing each other, holding hands as the ocean whispered up the beach and foamed around their knees.

Her mouth dried, and she couldn't speak. Pictures flashed through her mind like a fast-forward movie: ice, snow hurtling toward her, frosty plumes of breath, the elevators at the Edelweiss, the gondola, skiers zigzagging across a cold white field. She swallowed and looked up at him with helpless eyes.

Grant stared deeply into her stricken gaze; then he stroked her cheek with the back of his hand. "I see," he said quietly.

As it had in Vail, the moonlight turned his eyes to a tawny golden color. Teddi watched as a hood seemed to descend, blanking his expression. "Please, Grant. I'm not saying no, I—I just..." She almost said "can't," then hastily made an amendment. "I'm just not ready to make any decisions yet."

"No decision *is* a decision, Teddi."

She so badly wanted him to understand. "I love you, Grant. You know that, don't you?"

"Yes," he said slowly. "And that's what makes this so damned hard to accept."

"You're talking as if I've made an irrevocable decision," Teddi said, a frantic note in her tone. "But I haven't."

He looked at her. "Yes, you have."

The finality in his voice made her heart rise to her throat. Teddi swallowed with difficulty. Behind her eyes came the threat of tears, hot and stinging. If he only knew what he was asking, then he'd understand why she hesitated.

"Look, Teddi." He stopped at the foot of the stairs leading up to the lanai. "There's one thing I want to know, okay?"

"Anything."

"Does your reluctance to marry me have anything to do with the fact that I'm a cripple?"

Shock drained the color from Teddi's eyes. Her mouth dropped open. She stared into his expressionless gaze, but she wasn't deceived. The vulnerability she'd sensed in Vail surfaced with devastating intensity.

"Oh, my God," she whispered when she could speak. "Grant, no!" She clasped his hands and stared at him, her heart in her eyes. "You're not a cripple! There isn't anything anyone can do that you can't do. I had no idea you saw yourself that way. But it isn't true!" He stared at her. Earnestly, Teddi implored him with her eyes and hands. "Grant, my reluctance to marry you has nothing whatsoever to do with you. I *love* you. It has to do with me. *I'm* the cripple; don't you understand that?''

The words hung in the dark air. And suddenly she realized they were true. She was crippled. Unable to do what she most wanted.

His silence hurt more than recriminations would have.

''Grant? Please, let's not end it like this.'' Until she heard herself speak those words, she hadn't accepted his statement that she'd made a decision. But now she understood that she had. And she hated herself.

''Teddi . . .''

Desperation trembled along her body and edged her tone. ''Make love to me, Grant. Please? I need you so much.''

''Come here,'' he said roughly.

But it didn't work. For the first time since they'd found each other, the lovemaking was less than satisfactory. Though they came together with passion and tenderness, the loving possessed a desperate quality. And there was something almost melancholy in the lingering kisses and quiet touches.

She clung to him, trying to memorize the hard sweep of his muscles, the scent of mint and musk that was unique to him. And over his shoulder she stared at the clock, wanting to push back the dawn.

NEITHER SPOKE MUCH during the hour-long drive across the island to Kahului Airport. Teddi felt numb, protected by a strange lassitude that drained away all emotion. She followed Grant through check-in and waited beside him at the gate until his flight was called. She felt like a sleepwalker, stiff and wooden and unable to function normally.

"Well," Grant said when the public-address system announced boarding. His hands gripped her shoulders. "Goodbye, Teddi."

"You'll call or write...won't you?" She looked into his hard face and quiet eyes and felt her heart breaking into fragments.

"No," he said gently. Pride knotted his jaw. "I won't beg you."

"I didn't mean that," Teddi said hastily. "But surely you aren't going to just walk out of my life."

He kissed her on the forehead. And he held her so tightly she couldn't breathe.

And then—he was gone. Teddi ran to the window and pressed her face to the glass. She hoped he would look back, but he didn't. He approached the passenger-loading ramp without a backward glance.

Teddi sank to a chair and buried her face in her hands. She'd lost him.

"YOU DIDN'T LOSE HIM," Carol Kokuna said crisply. "You threw him away." She swung her tennis racket at an imaginary ball. "Like an id-iot."

Irritation flashed in Teddi's eyes. She jerked the sweatband from her head and dropped it in her bag. "Come on, Carol. I don't need this." She latched the door to the court behind her and stomped up the path toward the hotel.

"Right," Carol answered cheerfully. "What you need is someone to shake some sense into you. Which I'm trying to do."

"Look, you don't know the whole story. I don't want to live in Vail, okay? I like it here."

"Sure. You like running up three sets of stairs when there's a problem on the third floor, right? You're crazy about living alone. Makes sense to me. Like spitting in the wind makes sense."

Teddi stopped. She hadn't realized anyone had noticed that she avoided the elevators. Her shoulders dropped, and she passed a hand over her eyes. "Let's just forget it, okay? It's over." After two weeks of watching the mail and staring at her phone, she'd finally accepted that Grant wasn't going to contact her.

"If it's over, then why are you so miserable? You look like hell, by the way." Carol grinned. "I look terrific by comparison. All those lusty tourists that usually give you the big rush are begging to spend their money on little ole me."

Teddi managed a smile. "So let them."

"I am. I owe it to the island's reputation for hospitality."

They pushed into the locker room, showered and dressed. When they were seated in the Alii's air-conditioned lounge, sipping frosty piña coladas, Carol continued.

"Seriously, Teddi. I'm worried about you. What's wrong?"

"Everything," Teddi blurted out. She sighed. "Simply everything."

"Want to talk about it?"

Carol's concern raised a film of tears on Teddi's eyes. Lately she seemed to be overreacting to everything, wearing her emotions on her sleeve.

"I've been a fool," she said quietly.

"So? Who hasn't been a fool at one time or another? An old kahuna once said, 'There's no disgrace in acting the fool. The disgrace lies in continuing to act foolishly.'" When Teddi raised a skeptical eyebrow, Carol shrugged. "Well, if he didn't say that, he should have."

Teddi nodded. "It isn't just Grant, although he's a big part of it," she said, feeling her way. "It started years before I met him." Briefly, she sketched her background for Carol, omitting nothing. "So I ran away," she finished.

Carol's dark eyes widened. "*You?* I can't believe it. I've never seen you back down from a problem. In fact, you tackle problems you don't need to.''

"Oh, I'm terrific in my professional life," Teddi commented bitterly. "But not in my personal life." She released a breath. "And I'm not so sure about my professional life. What happens when the new wing is added to the Alii? Am I going to run up twenty-eight flights of stairs? What will happen to my professional life then? Are the owners going to want an executive administrator who can't ride an elevator?''

"You've got a problem, friend." Carol signaled the waiter to bring fresh drinks.

"Elevators aren't the problem; they're only one symptom. The problem is the past. My damned past is keeping me away from everything I want in life." Teddi's hands gripped into fists. "It's destroying what Grant and I had, it's costing my parents their retirement years, and eventually it will ruin any job opportunities I might have."

Carol narrowed her eyes and lit a cigarette. "And?''

"And I'm letting it happen," Teddi admitted miserably. She stared at a point in space while the impact of her admission swept over her. She didn't know what to do. She'd made an honest effort to beat the past; she'd tried. And she had failed. Frustration lined her brow.

Staring into her drink, she thought hard. "I failed because I didn't try for me," she said slowly, testing the truth. "I tried to beat the past for Grant's sake, not mine."

"Beg pardon?"

A dawning comprehension grew behind Teddi's eyes. "Don't you see, Carol? If I'm going to succeed in facing down the past, I have to do it for *my* sake. Because I *want* to, not to impress Grant or anyone else, but because I truly want to salvage my life!"

"I don't know what you're saying, but I think I agree."

"I'm not a quitter, dammit! I'm better than that."

"Teddi, no one ever said you were a quitter."

"And I'm through running away. I'm finished being an emotional cripple. I deserve to be happy as much as anyone else!" She stared at Carol as if defying Carol to protest.

Carol raised her hands and laughed. "I'm on your side, remember?"

"I love Grant Sterling. And I want a life with him." She wanted that more than anything else in the world. More than her job, more than the island's balmy breezes, more than anything. She wanted Grant Sterling enough to face down her past and reclaim her life.

"Now you're coming to your senses, friend."

"I've been telling myself I love it here for so long I almost convinced myself." Teddi shook her head, marveling. "But you know something? I miss autumn. And white Christmases. And I miss gorgeous crisp days with snow in the air and a sultry breeze of about two degrees below zero." She flattened her hand on the table and grinned. "Maui is a great place to visit, Carol, but I wouldn't want to live here forever."

"Are you serious?"

Teddi pushed to her feet. "I'm going to take your old kahuna's advice. I'm going after him."

"Right now?"

"Right now." Teddi laughed. Suddenly everything was light and bright and possible again. "It's been weeks since Grant left, miserable weeks." A radiant smile erased the faint circles beneath her eyes. "Will you sell my house and ship my things to Vail?"

"You know I will, but...Teddi? Are you sure?"

"I've never been more sure of anything in my life. I'm going home." Tears of happiness sparkled in her eyes. "Where I belong."

Chapter Thirteen

"Teddi!" Marta's eyes widened in astonishment; then her face crinkled into a joyful smile. She dashed from behind the registration counter and ran toward the door where Teddi stood brushing the snow from her cap and parka.

"Hans, Hans, come quick! Teddi's home!" Marta enfolded her in an embrace, then pulled back to stare into Teddi's laughing eyes, at the same time brushing back Teddi's hair. "It's only been two months since— What's wrong? Is anything wrong? Why didn't you tell us you were coming? Did you lose your job? Are you feeling well?"

Laughing, Teddi raised a hand, then hugged both her parents. "Nothing's wrong; I feel fine, and I didn't lose my job. I quit."

"You quit?" Hans asked. Bending, he scooped up Teddi's luggage and pushed it behind the desk. He propped a "closed" sign on the counter, and the lodge came to an unprecedented standstill as he led his daughter to a seat before the fireplace and ordered hot buttered rum for everybody in the lobby. "We're celebrating," he shouted happily. "My Teddi's home."

"Is it true? You've come home for good?" Tears of happiness wet Marta's cheeks as she pulled off Teddi's gloves and rubbed her cold fingers.

"I'm home, Mama. For good." She met her parents' eyes and hoped to heaven that it would all work out. If wanting and determination counted for anything, then it would. Gritting her teeth, she glanced at the hard pellets of snow blowing past the windows, and she scrubbed a hand over her frozen cheeks. This time she was going to beat the past.

"Marta, call Grant," Hans said. A knowing smile lit his expression. "That boy hasn't been the same since he came back from Maui. Wait until he hears you've come home!"

"No!" Teddi threw out a hand and stopped her mother from rising. She looked at them both, her voice conveying the urgency of her request. "I don't want him to know I'm here, not yet." A long breath expanded her chest, then released in a rush. "There are some things I have to do," she said quietly. "And I have to do them alone."

They looked at each other and then at Teddi. And finally, although she saw in their expressions that they didn't entirely agree, they both nodded.

Hans took her hand and cleared his throat. "Theodora, I know this has been hard on you. And on us, too. Losing Peter... and Kip. It isn't our place to ask why; we can only go forward. Do you understand?"

"Yes," Teddi whispered.

"For a long time neither your mother nor I could enter Peter's room. Did you know that?" Teddi hadn't. She looked at the pain in his eyes, and her heart contracted. "Then we talked it over and decided to put aside our anger and hurt. We decided just to be grateful for the time he was with us."

Marta nodded. "Life goes on, honey," she said gently. She touched Teddi's cheek and looked into her eyes. "Would Peter or Kip have wanted you to be unhappy? Or were they the kind of men to wish you well? To wish you every happiness life has to offer?"

Blinded by tears, Teddi opened her arms to embrace them. They had understood all along. They'd been there waiting to help when the time was right, when Teddi was ready. And now she was. Wiping the tears from her eyes, she smiled radiantly. "Tell me about your retirement," she said. "Where are you going when I take over the Edelweiss?"

Her question occasioned more tears from Hans, who turned aside to blow his nose and murmur something about catching a cold. Then Marta shyly withdrew a travel folder from one of her bulging apron pockets and spread it across her lap. In a few minutes she and Hans were arguing affectionately whether they should return to Switzerland first or bask in the sun on the Mediterranean. Teddi watched and listened with a broad loving smile. She was home.

"Oh, my goodness!" Marta laid a hand on her cheek, and her eyes rounded. "What time is it? Grant's coming to dinner, remember?"

Hans jumped to his feet, getting into the spirit of the deception. "Upstairs, quickly. He'll be here any minute; he's just downstairs."

Downstairs. Teddi closed her eyes and felt him with all her senses. A temptation to abandon her plan and run downstairs and fling herself into Grant's arms overwhelmed her. Then she swallowed hard and renewed her resolve. She'd been through this once with Grant; it wasn't fair to lean on him again. She knew in her heart that she had to face her problems alone. That was the only way she could hope to succeed.

Taking the steps two at a time, she dashed up the stairs to her room. But she couldn't resist. Following her heart, she stole down the hallway and stood on the balcony overlooking the lobby, concealing herself near the coatrack.

She saw him immediately, and her breath caught in her throat. He was standing where she'd first seen him, near the registration desk, talking to

Marta. The light above the desk shone on his hair, turning it a coppery-rust color. Hungrily, Teddi stared at him, wanting him, needing him. She absorbed every detail, yearning toward him as he turned to offer his arm to Marta. Her eyes darted over his strong craggy face, his wide shoulders and sensual lips. And she saw that he looked tired, and he was leaning heavily on his cane.

"Soon," she whispered, her fingers tightening on the balcony railing. "Soon, my darling."

IT WAS ONE THING to make brave promises—quite another to act on them. Teddi stood at her bedroom window, staring down at the snowplow shoveling out the parking lot. Even from this distance she could see the operator's breath puffing out in front of his lips. The radio had stated the temperature as a bitter-cold three degrees below zero. Not that the temperature discouraged the skiers. She could see brightly colored dots flashing across the face of the mountain.

"Where do I begin?" For one terrible moment she was overwhelmed by the task before her. Then she straightened her spine and turned to examine the trophies and plaques above her bed. Her blue eyes narrowed in determination. All she had to do was reach down inside and pull up the courage she'd had when she'd faced some of the toughest competition in the nation. She hadn't run away then. She'd had the grit to see it through and win. And, by God, she still had it. Character didn't vanish.

Squaring her shoulders, Teddi stared hard at the collection of trophies and ribbons and clippings. Then she marched downstairs and positioned herself in front of the elevator before she could change her mind. The doors whooshed open—then closed. And she cursed herself.

She was going to do this. Her hands clenched and a film of light moisture appeared on her brow. Another elevator opened and closed as a tremor began in her toes and rippled upward. She ground her teeth.

Then she made herself dash blindly into the next open door. The doors closed behind her with a solid clunk, and her eyes widened in panic. Worse, the elevator didn't move. She couldn't get out. The air would vanish, and she couldn't escape!

Sucking air deeply into her lungs and thanking God there were no other passengers, Teddi forced herself to reach out and jab a button. The elevator ascended silently as she pressed herself against the wall and told herself she wouldn't be crushed and there would be enough air. At the eighth floor the doors opened, and Teddi smiled sickly at the man and woman who stepped inside. She rode to the lobby with them.

For two days she rode the elevators. Eventually she learned to grade herself on a number system. Ten represented the ultimate fear; one was no fear at all. For reasons Teddi didn't understand, the system helped. Her fear became more manageable when assigned a number value. At the end of the third day she presented herself in the lodge kitchen and waited for a room-service order from the top floor. When it came, she volunteered to make the delivery and calmly pushed the cart onto the service elevator.

"Three," she whispered proudly when she returned. A wide smile transformed her features. "A three!" She'd started with a shivering, quaking ten and ended with a righteous three.

She followed her initial triumph by enduring two hard days of riding the gondola up and down Vail Mountain. And when she could step out of the car with a score of three or less, she grinned, then visited nearby hotels and rode their elevators until the security staff began casting her suspicious glances.

"I'm so proud of you," Hans said at dinner. If he'd had his way, he would have made a general announcement to anyone who would listen.

Teddi glowed. But the hardest part was yet to come. That night, she slowly approached the storage closet where her skis were kept. After a long hesitation she opened the padlock and removed her skis and boots. A line of anxiety creased her brow before she forcibly smoothed it away. Keeping her thoughts carefully blank, she cleaned the skis and waxed them, then propped them beside her bedroom door.

After her morning exercises she began slowly by strapping on her boots, then stepping into the ski bindings. The first day she didn't leave her room. Grinding her teeth, she snapped in and out of her skis, holding her breath and concentrating on scoring the degree of dread and anxiety that drenched her body in sweat.

On the second day she repeated the process outside, behind the Edelweiss. And it was all right. Not terrific but all right.

On the third day she sidestepped up the small hill below her bedroom window. At the top she drew a long, slow breath, held it until her heart thundered, then released it in a rush.

She couldn't make herself lean forward. Her body was tensed and ready. The distance couldn't have been more than twenty feet. But she couldn't do it.

"Get tough, dammit." She ground her teeth and gripped her poles until her knuckles whitened beneath her gloves. A tiny voice whispered in her ear: *This is a nine.* Teddi listened to her pulse thudding wildly in her ears. "You're tough, Ansel," she said firmly, not believing it. "Plenty tough."

Then she hurled herself forward. She zipped down the hill and fell in a pile at the bottom. But she'd done it. Untangling herself, she stared up at the single row of tracks leading down the minuscule hill. Her heart soared, and her lips broke into a wide, elated smile. She'd done it!

Four days later she looked at her father across the dinner table and inquired as casually as a wide grin would permit. "Dad? If you can spare an hour or two tomorrow, would you like to go skiing?"

Hans and Marta jumped from their chairs and rushed around the table to hug her and then each other. "I'd love to," Hans enthused. "We'll start with the beginners slopes and then—"

"No," Teddi interrupted. "I've already skied the beginners slopes and the intermediates." She met her father's grin. "Let's take Simba."

"Simba?" It was Vail's most advanced run. Hans and Marta looked at each other.

"It's true," Marta whispered, tears of happiness hanging on her lashes. "You're really home. For good."

"For good. I have my life back." And she knew it was the life she wanted. Leaning forward, she took her parents' hands. "And you two have some wonderful years ahead, too—" Teddi smiled "—if you can get used to slowing down and not working so hard."

Her parents exchanged a long glance, and Teddi frowned above her smile. She knew that look; they were deciding something. Long years of marriage and affection made words unnecessary. "Mom?" she asked. "Dad?"

Hans cleared his throat, then covered her hand. "There's something we should tell you."

"We would have told you earlier, but we didn't want to worry you," Marta added, patting Teddi's cheek.

She looked from one to the other, feeling her heart skip a beat. Whatever they had kept secret was serious; she saw that much in their concerned eyes. Teddi wet her lips. "Tell me."

"It's my heart . . ."

Teddi sat frozen as Marta, with interruptions from Hans, told of the heart attack a year ago and a long hospital stay, of the pills she now carried in her bulging apron pocket. As the story unfolded, a variety of emotions crossed Teddi's face and tugged at her heart. Fear, love, guilt, anxiety.

She squeezed Marta's hand so tightly her mother laughed and protested. To Teddi's eyes, Marta suddenly looked her age and more vulnerable than Teddi had ever imagined. She had always thought of her parents as indestructible; the realization that they were not brought tears rushing to her eyes.

"Now, now, dear, you mustn't cry." Marta cast a quick look at Hans as she leaned to place her arm around Teddi. "I'll be fine," she managed through a misty smile.

"The doctor says your mother will outlive us all," Hans quickly interjected, "if she'll take her medicine and stop overdoing."

"Stop overdoing," Teddi repeated in a whisper, staring at them. The only way Marta would relax her schedule at the inn was if—Dear God. Teddi closed her eyes and swallowed a dark taste. What if she hadn't come home? What if she'd never faced down the barriers of her past? "You should have told me," she managed, speaking around the lump in her throat. "I would have come home earlier."

"Theodora, we wanted you home because this is where you want to be, not because of some obligation or sense of duty."

Teddi nodded and smiled at them through moisture-filled eyes. She wasn't certain she agreed with their reasoning, but it didn't surprise her. That's how they were. She kissed them both and held the embrace with Marta for a long moment. After she'd asked questions, eliciting all the details of her mother's condition, and had insisted that Marta rest in the afternoons now that she was home, a sudden thought struck Teddi.

"Grant. Does Grant know?"

Marta nodded. "I made him promise not to tell you." She filled their coffee cups from the pot on the table.

"He wanted to." Hans agreed vigorously.

Anger flickered behind Teddi's eyes. "He should have."

"That's what he said," Marta admitted. Her soft fingers brushed Teddi's cheek. "Don't be angry, honey. He wouldn't be worthy of loving if he were a man to break his promises."

At her mother's words, surprise widened Teddi's eyes. "You know?"

They both laughed. "Of course we know. And we couldn't be happier for you both." Wearing the smile of a satisfied matchmaker, Marta gave Teddi a motherly nudge. "Isn't it time you told him you're home?" she asked gently.

"Almost." Teddi's heart soared at the thought of seeing Grant again, of feeling his strong arms around her. "But first—Simba. Will you come with me, Dad?"

"You know I will. With pride and pleasure."

They skied Simba twice on the coldest day of the year.

And it was wonderful. Exhilarating, intoxicating.

At the foot of the hill, Hans wrapped her in a bear hug. "I'm so proud of you! You looked just like you did six years ago. You've barely lost any of your form or speed." Arm in arm they gazed up at the mountain. "You beat it, Theodora. You're free now."

But she wasn't, not yet. There was still something she had to do.

Teddi slipped from bed the next morning as the sun was peeping over the mountain. She dressed hurriedly in the chill morning air, then found the box she'd prepared the night before and slipped it into her backpack. Stepping outside, she strapped on her skis, then cast a quick glance at the cold, crisp sky before she pushed off.

Moving with long, regular strides, establishing an even breathing pattern, Teddi moved cross-country toward Pine Overhang. Inhaling deeply, she breathed the fresh, sharp scent of spruce and pine and felt the wind and temperature painting her cheeks red.

She was breaking the cardinal rule for cross-country skiing, which insisted that skiers travel in pairs. But when she arrived at Pine Overhang, she knew her instincts to come alone had been correct.

Cutting to a halt, she silently stared at the smoothly rounded pack where the snow flowed over rocks and debris deposited by the avalanche on the day six years ago. And her eyes turned upward, seeing it again, that terrible rumbling mass roaring toward her.

She passed a hand over her eyes and shook her head until once again the day was bright and clear and silent.

Kneeling, Teddi swung her backpack around to the front and removed the box. Then she pressed her lips together and sidestepped up the side of the snow mound until she stood on top. She waited quietly until her hands had ceased to tremble.

"I love you both," she said softly. Tears formed on her lashes, then spilled. "With all my heart I wish you were here today." Tilting her head, she blinked hard at the sky, then at the mountain. "I want you to know that I will always love you. And I'll never forget." She swallowed the hot tightness in her throat, and her voice sank to a whisper. "But now it's time to say goodbye."

Opening the box, Teddi removed two sprays of red roses and laid them gently on the snow.

She looked back once at the two splashes of scarlet vivid against the glistening white snow; then she turned and leaned over her skis.

When she arrived back at the lodge, shadows were dappling the slopes, and the sun was slipping toward the peaks.

"Mom?" Teddi warmed her hands before the fire. "Mom, would you wait forty minutes, then call Grant?" Marta's face broke into a wreath of smiles. "Tell him to step out on his balcony and look toward Nichol Run."

SHE SAW THE LIGHTS in Grant's windows as she flew into Nichol's forth turn, and she could almost hear his phone ringing as she guided her skis off the slope and into the stand of pines.

And then he was standing on his balcony, a puzzled look drawing his brows together as he stared toward the point where Nichol swept into the curve before plunging on down the mountain.

She skied toward him, her red cap and parka a moving dot of color beneath the deepening shadows below the pines.

"Teddi? Teddi!"

She was laughing and crying and calling his name. And then she was in his arms, and they were falling in the snow, rolling in it, tumbling in it, a tangle of legs and skis and poles.

But she didn't feel the cold snow tingling on her face, she felt nothing but the hard beat of Grant's lips on hers, the hungry weight of his body and the tears of joy spilling through her laughter.

"Happy Valentine's Day," she said, lying in the snow, looking into his wonderful tawny eyes. "I brought you a heart."

Chapter Fourteen

Wrapped in towels, they lay on the carpet before a crackling fire. Her eyes softly glowing from the aftermath of lovemaking, Teddi reached out a hand to stroke his cheek, reassuring herself that she wasn't dreaming.

Grant caught her hand and placed a kiss in her palm. "Tell me again how long you've been here."

"Two weeks." She drew his fingertips toward her and kissed each one.

"That explains it."

"Explains what?" Rolling onto her stomach, Teddi stretched toward the wine bottle and refilled their glasses.

"Why you didn't answer my letter."

"What letter?"

A lopsided grin displayed a flash of white teeth. "I caved in. I wrote you a long, angry letter telling you I'd wait forever if that's how damned long it took." When Teddi grinned and arched a teasing eyebrow, he smacked her lightly on her toweled bottom and laughed. "I wasn't happy about it."

"That makes it all right, then. Your moment of weakness is forgiven." She smiled and traced the little lines radiating from the corner of his eye with her fingertip. "Does this mean we're a 'regular thing,' I believe you called it?"

"Well..." He drawled the word, dragging it into two syllables. "I don't know, Ansel." He rolled on his back and crossed his hands on his chest. "I'll have to think about it." He cast her a sidelong glance. "This is all happening so fast..."

Teddi lifted on top of him and wriggled a finger under his nose. "Listen to me, Sterling. I didn't go through all this to have you turn wishy-washy on me. Now, think it over, and think it over fast. Are we serious or not?"

His smile sobered, and he gazed into her eyes. "Did you ski again for me, Teddi?"

"No," she answered softly. "For me. This time for me. Because I wanted my life back."

"And are you free now?" His arms closed around her waist, and he held her tightly against his body.

"Almost. So..." Her warm breath flowed in his ear as she trailed teasing kisses along his temple, his earlobe, and then followed his strong jaw to the pulse at his throat. "So...have you decided yet?"

He chuckled softly. "Convince me."

"Playing hard to get, huh?" Teddi nipped his shoulder. Then she ran her hands down his chest to the edge of the towel and fumbled it open. "Have you decided yet?"

His hand found her breasts beneath the towel and rolled her nipples into aching need. "Do you, Teddi Ansel, promise never to drown a perfectly good steak in gallons of A-1 Sauce?"

"I do."

"And do you promise to get up when the alarm buzzes? Cheerfully and without complaint?"

She pulled back and a made a face. "Never."

"Hmm. Would you at least promise not to snore?" His hands spread an electric warmth over her buttocks as he positioned her on top of him.

"I promise to try. Have you decided yet?"

"You're merciless," he murmured in a husky growl as his mouth closed over her nipple, kindling an explosion of heat.

Teddi moaned softly. "Yes," she whispered. Her fingers curled over the muscles tensing on his shoulders, and she buried her face in the warm crease at his neck.

Gathering her in his arms, Grant rolled over so she lay beneath him. Stroking her silken hair back from her face, he gazed deeply into her eyes. "I love you, Teddi Ansel. And this is a 'regular thing' until you're ready for the next step."

"I love you, Grant Sterling," she whispered. Radiance lit her eyes, and her body trembled with joy. "Oh, Grant, I love you so much."

His mouth covered hers in a hard kiss of possession. Teddi's lips parted in surrender, and tears of happiness sparkled on her lashes. And when their lovemaking reached a fiery crescendo, she called his name and blinked in wonder, marveling that such joy existed.

Later, when they lay curled in each other's arms in Grant's bed, she felt the warm flow of his breath stirring her hair.

"Grant? Are you awake?" Turning, Teddi faced him across the pillow, looking deeply into his moonlit eyes. "There's still one thing I have to do," she said softly. "One last piece of unfinished business."

A puzzled frown darkened his gaze before he understood. He stroked her hair. "All things have a season, my love. Time won't turn backward." Gently, he pulled her close, and she felt his knee against her own. "Some things can't be conquered—they can only be accepted."

"If I don't try, I'll always wonder. I have to know," she said against his lips. "Will you help me?"

After a brief hesitation, he murmured, "You know I will. I'll arrange everything." After kissing her, he stared into her eyes. "How much time do you need?"

She thought hard. Mid-April was the outside date. After that point the surface snow would begin to melt. "Two months from today," she decided, knowing it wasn't enough time, not nearly enough. "The second week in April."

Already she was planning her training regimen.

IT WAS BITTER COLD. Colder than the records noted for the downhill race at Lake Placid. Teddi stamped her feet and blew on her fingers and stared at the flags spaced down the face of the mountain. They snapped and fluttered in the breeze.

"The final standards of battle," she murmured beneath her breath. A silvery mist formed before her lips.

"What did you say, Theodora?"

She stared at her father, who was examining her skis with a practiced eye. "Am I being silly, Papa?" She looked at her friends talking and laughing over the cups of hot coffee Marta was passing, and she suddenly wondered if she was acting wisely. Perhaps this part of the past should remain buried. Perhaps, as Grant had suggested, the season was past, never to come again.

Hans straightened and looked at her. "Only you can answer that, my little Theodora." His mitten brushed the heat in her cheeks. "Only you know what is necessary."

Teddi gazed at the flags and the mountain. How many times had she bolted out of a nightmare, drenched in sweat, after having dreamed she was there? At Lake Placid. At the Olympics. How many times had she asked herself if she could have taken the gold?

Frowning, she looked down at her boots. She had dreamed of winning from the time she was a starry-eyed adolescent. She'd seen the gold medal in her mind, planned where she would keep it, directed all her energies toward winning.

But then, when the time came, she had walked away. As if it hadn't mattered. As if the gold medal were not important.

Was it? Now? She stared at the mountain and clenched her teeth.

"An old kahuna once told me that people could guarantee themselves happiness," she said softly. "Because each person has it within his power to take whatever steps are necessary to obtain that happiness."

But the old kahuna hadn't explained how to identify what made one happy.

Hans looked at her, then asked gently. "Will pretending make you happy?"

"I thought so," Teddi whispered. But now she wondered. She pushed her hands into the pockets of her parka and stared up at the flags snapping in the breeze, and her stomach tensed.

If she failed today, her friends would offer consolation by reminding her of the short training period. They would excuse her failure by pointing out that she couldn't regain her form in two months no matter how rigorously she had trained, not after a six-year absence.

And if she won—then would she castigate herself the rest of her life for rejecting Lake Placid? Would she be tempted to prove herself again and again?

Grant kissed her and pulled her cap down. "Okay, love, everything is ready."

She looked at him from expressionless eyes, feeling her nerves tighten. He wore the red parka she'd requested. So she could see him from the top of the run.

"The timekeeper is in the booth over there." Grant pointed a gloved finger. "The finish line is there, see it?"

Teddi nodded. Her hands clenched into fists in her pockets.

"You take the puma up to the starting gate. A man from the racing commission will start you. Okay?" He looked down at her, and Teddi saw the nervousness in his eyes.

"It's all right," she said quietly.

"Hans and I have duplicated everthing as nearly as possible to the conditions of Lake Placid. The angle of descent is the same, the slope here as close as anything in Vail."

She looked away from the love and anxiety in his eyes, choosing instead to stare at the red flags. And she loved him for caring so much, loved him with an intensity that ached inside.

"Teddi? We're ready when you are."

She nodded, studying the mountain, hating it for a moment. "Two practice runs, right?"

"That's it."

Turning, she looked at him, her eyes hard and her mind already at the top. "Let's go."

Grant held her for a long moment; then he kissed her. "Good luck."

She clung to him for the span of a heartbeat; then she began her final warm-ups, her gaze steady on the starting gate above the flags.

When she finished, Teddi stepped into her skis and waited as her father checked the bindings. When he finished, he straightened and clasped her hands, looking into her eyes. "Remember, stay relaxed. Keep your knees flexed and don't think about the timekeeper. Just take the gates one at a time. You can do it."

"Knees flexed . . . one at a time." Gliding slowly, easily, she approached the puma, caught the bar between her legs and rode it up to the starting gate.

The man inside grinned and gave her a thumbs-up sign.

Teddi nodded and positioned her skis on the starting mound, sliding them back and forth, seeking the perfect thrust point. Below her the flags cracked and flapped in the cold air. She could see her parents and her friends clustered near the finish line. And Grant.

"When you're ready," the man said, placing his finger on the button that would start the seconds ticking in the timekeeper's booth.

She drew a long breath. "Now." Teddi shouted, pushing off.

Wind rushed at her goggles, the mountain jarred through her legs, straining at her knees. She took the first gate wide, and cut too narrowly into the second. Concentration blown, she slid in and out of the gates, knowing it was a bad run.

At the foot of the mountain she lowered her poles and swished to a halt, her face expressionless.

Grant shouted something to the timekeeper, then rushed toward her. "A full six seconds off," he said.

"Damn." Teddi bit her lip. "I wouldn't even have made the trial with that kind of time."

"But you *did* make the trials," he reminded her.

"That's right." But it had been a long time ago. Mouth set, she turned toward the puma. This time she gripped her poles with hands that were moist beneath her gloves as she stared at the scarlet flags. "Okay, now!"

It was a good run—not great but good. Except she lifted her head too soon and crashed, spinning across the finish line on her bottom. When she stopped, Teddi clasped her hands around her legs and rested her head on her knees.

Instantly, Grant and Marta were at her side.

"Are you all right?" Grant asked.

Marta helped her to her feet. "You don't have to do this. It isn't necessary." She brushed the snow from Teddi's pants and parka.

Teddi looked into Grant's eyes and wet her lips. "This is it," she whispered. "Last chance."

"Go for it, Teddi." He smiled at her. "Bring home the gold."

She felt his eyes on her as she skied to the puma and hooked it between her legs. And then her mind cleared of everything but the flags and the mountain. Closing her eyes, she felt the cold breeze on her face, inhaled the scent of snow and pine.

It would have been like this at Lake Placid. The sun beginning to slip behind the clouds, and cold. The taste of spring snow in the air. Her nerves would have jumped on the surface of her skin as they were doing now; her stomach would have fluttered with excitement and anxiety.

Stepping fluidly from the puma, she skied slowly toward the starting gate. Easy now, nice and easy.

Relax. Knees flexed. Long deep breaths. Take the gates one at a time. As she always did, as she'd done a thousand times before.

Teddi slid into the starting booth and leaned into position, staring down the hill. And suddenly the clock spun backward. She was no longer on Vail Mountain, she was at Lake Placid. She could see the crowd below shading their eyes to look up at her; she could hear Peter's whisper in her ear: You can do it, squirt. You can take the gold.

Her eyes narrowed as she seated her goggles. This was it. The Olympics. And she was America's hope, the best downhill racer in the country. And today she could make her country proud.

She filled her lungs with a long, deep breath, held it, then exhaled slowly. She dangled her arms at her sides, staring down the hill; then she took her poles, holding them loosely. Leaning forward, her concentration total, she tensed her legs, feeling the strength flow through her body.

''Now!'' she shouted.

Her poles dug into the snow as she pushed over the mound, then tucked them up under her arms to gain the speed she wanted going into the first gate. She shot through the flags, skimming the pole with an inch to spare.

The run was going to be good. Very good. She could feel it as powerfully as she felt the mountain jolting up her legs, felt the fresh icy wind on her cheeks and her hair streaming behind her.

Best of all, this time she knew she had the edge, that elusive edge of excellence that occurred when the body relaxed and instinct took control. She flashed through the second gate, her body low and tight.

And she perceived the race in slow motion, that odd phenomenon of slowing time experienced by many professional athletes. When the sense of distorted time failed to occur, she knew she wasn't performing at her peak.

Exhilarated, Teddi felt as if she had all the time in the world. As the third gate vanished over her shoulder, she had time to realize that she was about to learn the truth. After all these years.

The fourth gate rushed toward her, and her knees shifted beneath her body. The flag winked past, a blur.

Or would she? A frown tightened her mouth. Did this race prove anything, or was she only refusing to face responsibility for her decision six years ago? And fighting to change it.

This wasn't Lake Placid. Her season, the one that had genuinely been hers, was gone. She couldn't recreate it. Or spin back the clock. She couldn't beat this portion of her past, it was too late—she could only accept it and go on.

The fifth gate opened before her, and Teddi crouched and leaned into a tight, crisp curve. The run was going to be one of her best—she sensed it with an instinct born of years and years of competitive training.

And it didn't matter.

The shock of comprehension jolted through her body. Behind her goggles her eyes widened, and she swept the next gate a foot wide.

It didn't matter if she won or lost. It wasn't important anymore.

Six years ago, her entire life had focused on skiing, on winning the gold. Now her focus centered on the people she cherished most. And she didn't have to prove herself to them.

All she had to do was accept. Once she fully accepted the past and quit fighting it, the nightmares would cease. She would never again hear the rumble of the avalanche, never again torment herself with visions of Lake Placid.

The next gate flew toward her.

Teddi watched it approach and understood she had come to terms with herself. And with the past.

Tears sparkled behind her goggles—whether from regret or relief, she would never know for certain. The sharp physical edge drained from her body, and motion speeded to normal time.

It was over. She knew it was finally over.

She entered the gate, but she didn't lean into the next curve. Instead, she angled straight through the flags and continued to the edge of the slope, slicing to a halt.

Below her, the screams and shouts of encouragement died to a puzzled silence. Pushing up her goggles, Teddi looked down at the cluster of friends and family waiting at the finish line. The timekeeper was staring at her, his mouth open. Hans and Marta were holding hands and smiling, their eyes moist with understanding.

Then she found Grant's red parka and cap. And the love softening his strong craggy face told her that he, too, understood. As she watched, he lifted his arms to her, and she blinked at the tears welling in her eyes. She had won. Her parents knew, and Grant knew. And do did she. She had won something far more valuable than any medal.

Pointing her skis down the slopes, Teddi glided slowly toward the finish line, skiing parallel to the remaining scarlet flags as a great weight lifted from her heart. She was free. She was finally free. The last residue from the past cracked and fell away.

When she glided to a stop, Kelly rushed forward. "What happened? Are you all right?"

"I'm fine," Teddi said, looking at Grant over Kelly's head. "For the first time in years, I'm really and truly fine."

"But your time," Kelly insisted, waving a mitten toward the timekeeper's booth. "If you hadn't stopped... at midpoint your time was—"

Teddi raised her hand. She met Grant's eyes. "The only gold I want is a wedding ring."

Grant caught her in his arms, and his warm mouth met her lips. "I'm so proud of you." His frosty breath melted over her lips.

"You were right," she whispered. "My season is past."

"It's our season now." Pulling off her mitten, he slid a gold ring on her finger. An enormous diamond solitaire winked up at her. "Say you'll marry me, Teddi."

"Yes. Oh, yes." Laughing and crying, Teddi gazed up at him, her eyes shining with a luminous glow as the first snowflakes gently pelted her cheek. She caught the next one on the tip of her tongue and laughed out loud.

"Ansel," Grant murmured huskily in her ear, "remember that bottle of first-best brandy? Well, I think I've found the perfect occasion for it. Let's go home."

Teddi laughed into his craggy face, into his warm, wonderful gaze that swept her face and made love to her. Before his mouth claimed her lips, she smiled into his golden-brown eyes and knew she had won everything that was important. Her life belonged to her again. And she knew exactly how she wanted to spend it. And with whom.

Epilogue

Grant leaned against the railing, feeling the cold from the ice rising to meet his smile. Amused, he watched his six-year-old daughter pick herself off the ice and brush her gloves across her fanny. Her small features knit into a frown of concentration that reminded him of Teddi. Still smiling, he watched Sunny gather herself, then glide across the ice, picking up speed until her skates flashed and her reddish-gold braids swung out from her sweater. This time she cut a perfect figure eight without falling and waved to him, her small face flushed with triumph.

Grinning broadly, Grant waved back, sharing the victory of her accomplishment.

"She's a natural, Grant." Eric Stroheim glided to a stop on the other side of the railing. "I've been coaching ice skaters for thirty-five years, and I can tell you honestly, I've seen only two others with Marta's innate ability and potential."

A father's pride constricted Grant's chest. "She comes by it naturally," he said lightly. Sunny possessed that indefinable something that set her apart from other skaters her age. Both he and Teddi had had the same quality once. Teddi still did. When she skied, other skiers stopped to watch. She had the mark of a champion, a graceful harmony of motion that was a true pleasure to observe.

"It would be tragic to waste that ability. I'd like to talk to you and Teddi about taking Marta out of skating classes and putting her into a serious training program." Grant watched as she tightened into a spin, her braids flying into a blur. Her coach was one of only a handful of people who referred to the child by her given name Marta, which Teddi insisted upon, after her mother.

"We could have her ready by the time she's fourteen," Eric urged.

Grant didn't need to ask what Eric meant. The Olympics. "That's a big commitment," he said softly.

Eric smiled. "She comes by it naturally." He pushed from the rail. "Think about it, okay? I'll drop by the lodge next week, and we'll talk."

Nodding thoughtfully, Grant watched Sunny gliding toward him, as at ease on the ice as if she'd been born with skates on her feet. His heart melted. This was how Teddi must have looked at that age.

Except for the eyes. Both Sunny and Peter had Grant's dark eyes.

"Hi, Daddy. Did you see me?" A smile as natural and radiant as Teddi's tilted up to him. Freckles dusted her nose; red and gold bangs fell across her forehead. Like her mother, she was going to be a beauty.

"I saw you," he said, swinging her over the railing for a hug before he set her down. "You were wonderful."

"Is it time to go? Already?"

"You've been here three hours. Aren't you getting hungry?" Bending, he unlaced her skates and helped her out of them.

"No." She looked toward the lights gleaming on the ice, and her eyes were shining. "I love to skate, Daddy. I want to be the best skater there ever was."

"Ever?" he teased.

"The best in the whole world," she said solemnly.

He took her hand. "Well, you can be. You can be anything you want to be. But it takes a lot of work."

"I know," she said with the airy wisdom of a six-year-old.

Grant laughed and squeezed her hand.

SOMETIMES TEDDI'S HAPPINESS was so great she had to pinch herself to believe she wasn't dreaming. Outside, the temperature was dipping toward a comfortable six degrees; she smiled at the thought. Inside the lodge a noisy group was singing around the fireplace and toasting late arrivals with tankards of hot buttered rum. Even the new wing was full this weekend, mostly with Denver people here to take advantage of the last good snow before spring.

Smiling, Teddi jotted a note on the margin of the register, then bent to her knees behind the counter. "Hi, big fella. It's about time to wash for dinner. Daddy and Sunny will be home soon."

Peter grinned up at her, his eyes twinkling with an ever-present mischief. "I'm already washed."

"Oh, no, you aren't." Teddi helped him pick up his Star Wars figures and put them in the basket. "Upstairs, young man. Ask Grandpa to put soap on the washcloth for you."

She ruffled his shock of reddish curls and watched him run up the staircase toward the family's quarters, remodeled last year. At four years old, Peter's features weren't yet set, but Teddi thought he would resemble Grant more than her. He had Grant's firm chin and dark eyes, and he would be tall like Grant.

But sometimes she looked at her son and saw traces of another Peter. Watching him run up the stairs, time blurred, and for a moment she watched another boy in another time. Teddi smiled, at last easy with her memories.

"Hello, beautiful." Grant's voice breathed in her ear, and she smelled the sharp, exhilarating scent of cold air and snow. "Think I can steal you away for a drink before dinner?"

Teddi gave him the special smile she saved just for him, then responded to the tug on her sleeve.

"Mr. Stroheim said I have natural talent, Mommy." A miniature version of herself looked up at Teddi. Excitement danced in her daughter's eyes. "And Lydie Myerson can come to my slumber party. Isn't that great?"

"Absolutely terrific. I want you to tell me all about it at dinner."

Grant slipped an arm around her waist, and they watched Sunny dash up the stairs. "So," Grant said, kissing the top of her head, "what did you do all day? Watch the soaps and eat bonbons?"

She smiled at their standard joke, then surrendered the registration desk to the night clerk. They chose a deep-cushioned love seat away from the noisy crowd by the fireplace and ordered wine spritzers.

Teddi rested her head against her husband's broad shoulder, pleased that she still experienced a thrill of anticipation at his touch. She suspected she always would. She laced her fingers into his, and her thoughts jumped ahead to the moment when they would snuggle into the big feather bed upstairs.

Speaking softly, they caught each other up on the day's activities. Grant had spent the morning with his head buyer, coordinating the addition of the new shop in Keystone; Teddi had skied the beginners' slopes with Peter, then attended a fashion show she'd arranged for the lunch crowd before taking over the front desk.

"Tough life, Ansel," Grant said laughing.

"Mrs. Sterling to you, fella." They smiled at each other, enjoying the moment.

"Uh-oh."

The words were hardly out of Grant's mouth when a shower of popcorn cascaded over the balcony and rained down onto the lodge floor. Two reddish-gold heads poked through the balcony rails, then vanished behind smothered giggles.

Teddi sighed and tried to look stern. "I think you should go upstairs and throttle your children."

"*My* children?" He blinked innocently. "I've never seen those two rascals in my life. I have no idea who they are."

"Uh-huh. Strange—they look just like you."

"Do you think so?" He looked enormously pleased.

"Definitely." She kissed his chin. "You throttle, I'll sweep up, and we'll meet in the dining room in ten minutes. Okay?"

The table they chose for dinner was near the kitchen door so that Teddi could keep an eye on things—although she didn't need to when Hans and Marta were in Vail. Hans would hardly let her do a thing.

"It seems to me that waiter isn't as attentive as he might be," Hans said, glancing over the dining room. "Maybe I should speak to him."

Marta smiled and exchanged a look with Teddi. "Now Hans, you're retired, remember?" After pressing Teddi's hand, Marta rescued her namesake's glass of milk before it tumbled off the edge of the table. "I understand you and Peter showered the guests with popcorn."

Sunny smiled beneath a sweep of golden lashes. "Grandpa told us how to do it. He said Mama and Uncle Peter used to do it, too."

"Hans! You didn't," Marta said while Grant laughed and Hans looked sheepish. He winked at Sunny and Peter, who exchanged conspiratorial grins.

"I know nothing about this," Hans insisted, raising his hands while the children laughed.

Teddi met Grant's eyes across the table, taking pleasure from the laughter in his gaze. Finally, her husband had a family of his own. Grant had been present at Sunny's and Peter's birth and had wept with joy the first time he held them. The love in his eyes as he smiled around the table made her heart swell and ache with happiness.

When they had sold Grant's house and moved into the lodge, she had worried that he might miss the privacy and solitude of his home. Instead, he had taken to innkeeping with cheerful exuberance, treating the guests as an extended family. The guests loved it and returned year after year.

When the conversation had moved on to a discussion of the latest Disney movie and cherry strudel and coffee had been served, Teddi touched Marta's hand. "How are you feeling, Mom?"

"Fit as a fiddle," Marta answered promptly. "Never better."

In one of fate's twists, Hans and Marta had bought a beach house in Maui. They spent most of the winter there and visited Grant and Teddi in time to ski before the melt; then it was on to Europe or wherever fancy took them. Marta's Maui tan contrasted handsomely with her white hair, and she looked healthy and younger than she had when Teddi had first come home.

"I love you, Mom," Teddi said softly. She looked at her own children, then leaned to kiss Marta's cheek. She had never appreciated her mother more than when she had become a mother herself.

Marta looked at her closely. "How are *you* feeling? You're not trying to do everything yourself, are you?"

Teddi laughed. "I love it." It was true. She couldn't imagine how she had ever envisioned a different life. The lodge by itself provided a constant source of challenge and variety; then there were Grant's shops, expanding into all the major ski areas, and good friends, and Peter and Sunny. And Grant. She smiled at him across the length of the table, enjoying the play of candlelight through his russet hair, loving the strength in his face, the warmth in his eyes. "I wouldn't change a thing," she said with a quiet smile.

Later, in the newly remodeled master suite, Teddi brushed her hair and listened as Grant repeated Eric Stroheim's recommendations for Sunny.

"She seems so young to begin such a vigorous training program," Teddi said, lowering her hairbrush and watching as Grant stretched out on the bed and crossed his arms behind his head. She never tired of looking at him, loving his long, hard athlete's body, the twinkle in his eye, the few strands of gray appearing at his temples.

"She wants to be the best, Teddi. Eric thinks she can be."

Teddi looked at him. "Everything comes full circle, doesn't it?" she asked softly, remembering the first time she had experienced the thrill of flying down the mountain, the first time she had thought of serious competition. Closing her eyes, Teddi pictured Sunny on the ice, thinking about Sunny's grace and astonishing ability. And she had seen the longing in her daughter's eyes when Sunny gazed at Teddi's and Grant's trophies. Her daughter's season was beginning.

After she and Grant had discussed the long road stretching ahead, Teddi said, "Well, if it doesn't work out, she can always quit." She looked at Grant whose twinkling eyes told her he knew what she would say next. "Except she won't quit, will she?"

"No, she won't quit." Grant met her eyes with quiet warmth. "Someday Sunny will take the gold."

Teddi nodded. Deep instinct told her Grant was right. "I guess all we can do is be there when the going gets tough and help her all we can."

"We will." He ran his eyes over the contours of her robe, and his voice deepened. "Come to bed, Mrs. Sterling. I want to talk to you about your eyes."

"My eyes?" Laughing, Teddi stretched on top of him and wound her fingers through his hair, smiling down into his face.

"They remind me of—"

"Columbines in spring?"

"Something like that." He kissed her deeply. "How would you feel about us having another baby?"

Teddi smiled, loving him. "If it was up to you, you'd fill every room in the lodge with little Sterlings." He happily agreed. "May I point out that we already have a boy and a girl?"

"Well, we need a spare." He rolled on top of her and eased her robe off one shoulder, kissing her exposed throat. "Someday Sunny and Peter might get married and leave home. Have you thought about that?"

She pretended to consider, teasing him. "You have a point," she admitted finally. Her arms tightened around his neck, and she laughed softly. "A spare?"

"Or two," he murmured against her lips. "Agreed?"

In answer, Teddi opened her robe farther, and her lips parted eagerly beneath his. It was definitely a first-best brandy night.

Readers rave about Harlequin American Romance!

What readers say about Harlequin romance fiction...

"I absolutely adore Harlequin romances!
They are fun and relaxing to read, and
each book provides a wonderful escape."
—N.E.,* Pacific Palisades, California

"Harlequin is the best in romantic reading."
—K.G.,* Philadelphia, Pennsylvania

"Harlequins have been my passport to the
world. I have been many places without
ever leaving my doorstep."
—P.Z.,* Belvedere, Illinois

"My praise for the warmth and adventure
your books bring into my life."
—D.F.,* Hicksville, New York

"A pleasant way to relax after a busy day."
—P.W.,* Rector, Arkansas

*Names available on request.

What the press says about Harlequin romance fiction...

"When it comes to romantic novels...
Harlequin is the indisputable king."
— *New York Times*

"...always with an upbeat, happy ending."
— *San Francisco Chronicle*

"Women have come to trust these
stories about contemporary people,
set in exciting foreign places."
— *Best Sellers*, New York

"The most popular reading matter of
American women today."
— *Detroit News*

"...a work of art."
— *Globe & Mail*, Toronto

The final book
in the trilogy by
MAURA SEGER

EDGE OF DAWN

*The story of the Callahans and Garganos
concludes as Matthew and Tessa must stand
together against the forces that threaten to
destroy everything their families have built.*

From the unrest and upheaval of the sixties
and seventies to the present, *Edge of Dawn*
explores a generation's coming of age
through the eyes of a man and a woman
determined to love no matter what the cost.

Available now wherever paperbacks are sold.

EDG-H-1-2R   **WORLDWIDE LIBRARY** ®

WORLDWIDE LIBRARY IS YOUR TICKET TO ROMANCE, ADVENTURE AND EXCITEMENT

Experience it all in these big, bold Bestsellers— Yours exclusively from WORLDWIDE LIBRARY WHILE QUANTITIES LAST

To receive these Bestsellers, complete the order form, detach and send together with your check or money order (include 75¢ postage and handling), payable to WORLDWIDE LIBRARY, to:

In the U.S.
WORLDWIDE LIBRARY
901 Fuhrman Blvd.
Buffalo, N.Y.
14269

In Canada
WORLDWIDE LIBRARY
P.O. Box 2800, 5170 Yonge Street
Postal Station A, Willowdale, Ontario
M2N 6J3

Quant.	Title	Price
_____	WILD CONCERTO, Anne Mather	$2.95
_____	A VIOLATION, Charlotte Lamb	$3.50
_____	SECRETS, Sheila Holland	$3.50
_____	SWEET MEMORIES, LaVyrle Spencer	$3.50
_____	FLORA, Anne Weale	$3.50
_____	SUMMER'S AWAKENING, Anne Weale	$3.50
_____	FINGER PRINTS, Barbara Delinsky	$3.50
_____	DREAMWEAVER, Felicia Gallant/Rebecca Flanders	$3.50
_____	EYE OF THE STORM, Maura Seger	$3.50
_____	HIDDEN IN THE FLAME, Anne Mather	$3.50
_____	ECHO OF THUNDER, Maura Seger	$3.95
_____	DREAM OF DARKNESS, Jocelyn Haley	$3.95

	YOUR ORDER TOTAL	$_____
	New York residents add appropriate sales tax	$_____
	Postage and Handling	$___.75
	I enclose	$_____

NAME _____

ADDRESS _____ APT.# _____

CITY _____

STATE/PROV. _____ ZIP/POSTAL CODE _____

WW-1-3